Flight Attendants want Love: Flying High with Jessica

Dirk Caldwell Romantic Erotic Novels, Volume 8

Dirk Caldwell

Published by Dirk Caldwell, 2023.

This is a work of fiction. Similarities to real people, places, or events are entirely coincidental.

FLIGHT ATTENDANTS WANT LOVE: FLYING HIGH WITH JESSICA

First edition. August 21, 2023.

ISBN: 979-8223699958

Written by Dirk Caldwell.

Also by Dirk Caldwell

Adventures of Stan
Stan does a Big Girl and gives her a Big Orgasm
Stan Does a Female Police Officer While On Duty
Stan Scores on a Booty Call with Barbara
Stan Takes Barb's Anal Cherry
Stan Teaches Oklahoma Karen About Sex in the City
Stan gets Kinky with Barb on Vacation
Barb Wants more Orgasms with Stan before She gets Engaged to Another Man
Stan Does Barbara's Mom!

Dirk Caldwell Romantic Erotic Novels
A Visit to the Farm with Darla - a Sexy Short Story
A Layover in Omaha with Tina
A Night in Eufaula with Lynn
A Trip to the Lake with Kim
Older Women need Love, too! Erika visits Atlanta
Lessons in Love: Gabriella visits Indianapolis
Big Girls Need Love, too! Barbara from Kokomo
Flight Attendants want Love: Flying High with Jessica
Back to the Farm with Darla - A Sexy Sequel
Redheads need Love: Megan from New Orleans

A Big Girl finds Love: Joann from Shreveport
Lust from London: My Affair with a British Nymphomaniac
Paula's Sexy European Weekend
Mother and Daughter Threesome

Dirk Caldwell Sexy Short Stories
To All the Girls I've Loved Before: Sexy Short Stories Book 1
To All the Girls I've Loved Before: Sexy Short Stories Book 2
To All the Girls I've Loved Before: Sexy Short Stories Book 3

Acknowledgment

Cover image by halayalex on Freepik
Back Cover generic airline pilot image by Blake Guidry at unsplash

Introduction

Jessica was laying on my hotel bed, her face flushed with excitement and lust at the idea of our first sexual experience. I had just pulled off her shorts and applied my tongue to her labia, tickling the clit and tasting the juices of her wet pussy. I moved up to position the head of my cock to her wet lips and prepared to enter her for the first time. Our eyes locked. When I pushed in, I didn't realize that this first time would begin a relationship that lasted decades. Let me tell you about how this happened.

My name is Dirk. Well, that's not my real name. I'd never be able to have a normal life if I used my real name. I was an airline pilot and single at the start of this encounter. I enjoyed being unencumbered and the benefits that came from that. I could travel the world as an international aircrew member and be with any woman I wanted without regret and have always enjoyed the freedom that came with that ability.

I love women. I noticed that some women and I had a powerful sexual attraction for some reason. Maybe it was that they intuitively knew I would give them the attention they yearned for. I'm not sure why it happened, for some reason some women get very aggressive when it comes to sex, and many wanted to try new things. I was happy to help. I have a lot of repeat customers, and just as many that wanted sex once and were satisfied with that. Even after giving my usual disclaimer that I am not looking for a long-term relationship, I've had some close calls.

A while back, I decided to write about my experiences. It's fun to recall with vivid detail the different women I've been with.

As a disclaimer, I always change enough of the information about the ladies so my writing could not possibly be traced back to them. Cities are changed, along with names, occupations, specific characteristics, branches of service for the military, etc. To do otherwise would not be gentlemanly. I do, however, mix in some of my local knowledge about locations. How did I get that information? Let your imagination be your guide.

New Hires

I had just finished my new hire ground school and simulator training at the airline and was scheduled for my initial operating experience flying the line with a supervisory pilot called a check airman. Assigned to the junior airplane of the fleet, the McDonnell Douglas MD-80 series, I was still getting used to the thing. I had a thousand hours or so in the Boeing 757 at my previous airline, and the -80 was a step back to a previous generation of airliners. Things that were automated in the 757 were manually controlled in the new (to me) plane. I was figuring it out, but slower than I wanted to.

Scheduling had assigned me to my first trip along with the check airman. It was a two-day trip, doing a round trip from Atlanta to Jacksonville, FL, then on to Buffalo, NY for our Remain Over Night (RON). The second day would reverse the route. I met the check airman the day prior, and he did a good job going over the myriad of things that a line pilot needs to know, but my head was spinning. With the show time agreed upon, we parted ways and I wanted to stick my head in a bucket of cold water to help my overheated brain.

I showed up in operations an hour early so I could take my time and pull up the needed flight information in the antiquated computer system. Then I checked my crew mailbox which was more like a cubbyhole for any relevant updates to manuals or navigation charts. I found the flight plan routes and folded my charts so fumbling would be kept to a minimum. I was ready to face the new plane and conquer it.

I met the smiling, silver-haired check airman and we went over the flight plan. Our plane was going to be at a far-out concourse, and check airman Les advised me to allow plenty of time to get out there, even using the airport shuttle train system. It was good advice. We left operations together and fully 15 minutes later arrived at the gate. Atlanta is a big airport.

Our plane had not arrived yet and was already putting us a few minutes behind schedule. For this first flight, Les would have to take time from his routine and do the walk-around inspection with me to sign me off to do it on my own on subsequent flights. We waited at the gate area off to the side, out of the way of the harried agents. Our flight attendants arrived, and we introduced ourselves, as did they. The lead flight attendant said she had a new hire on her first trip, and that was the first time I laid eyes on Jessica.

She was a tall, attractive young woman of about 30 years of age. She had brown hair long enough for her ponytail to come between her shoulder blades. Her smiling face was smooth and unlined, with pretty blue eyes and minimal makeup. She wore conservative earrings and a brand-new flight attendant uniform. Her chest showed the promise of nice boobs, and what I could see of her legs looked nice. She had broad, straight shoulders, and a slender, athletic swimmer's build. I realized I was staring at her. She was blushing.

I realized she was speaking. "Nice to meet another new hire, Dirk." She extended her hand, and it was warm and dry, with a firm handshake. She looked me in the eyes, still blushing.

"Nice to meet you, too, Jessica. This is my first flight in the MD-80, so hang on tight back there."

She laughed. "Call me Jess. I'll hold on tight! It's my first flight as a flight attendant!"

We all chatted about the schedule. The flight attendants would be with us all day, staying with us in Buffalo, and then would join another crew while we went to Jacksonville and back. For some reason, I was happy to hear they would be with us in Buffalo.

Our plane arrived, and Les and I headed down to do my walk-around training while the people were getting off. Completing that chore, we met the incoming crew and discussed the maintenance status. There were a few writeups in the logbook, but nothing prevented our flight. I hopped into the flight deck's right seat and stowed my gear while Les went back to brief the cabin crew. Already 10 minutes behind, we needed to load up the passengers in a hurry while preparing for the flight. Les wasn't pushing me, but I felt like I was behind.

The lead flight attendant Nancy leaned into the small flight deck and asked if I wanted anything to drink, so over my shoulder, I asked for a club soda as I was punching numbers into the flight management system. A couple of minutes later, I felt rather than saw someone behind me, and turned to see who it was. It was Jess, holding our drinks. I looked her in the blue eyes and thanked her. She blushed again. Maybe she just blushed a lot.

The gate agent came up and thrust a sheaf of paperwork at Les and asked to close the cabin door so we could record our departure time. We looked over the weight summary form and corrected the planned weight. I heard the entry door thump shut, and our ground crew called us on the interphone and told us he was ready. With Les' help, I called the ramp control and got us clearance to push back. It's different at every airport, and Atlanta was a madhouse. We were hot on the flight deck. The onboard air conditioning does not compete well with a Georgia summer day on the ground but works fine in the air. I was ready to get in the air and cool off.

We pushed back and started one engine to taxi. This saves fuel at the expense of extra engine air to run the air conditioning. There was a long conga line of planes waiting to take off, and it took at least a half hour to get to the end of the runway and take off. We started the second engine to give it time to warm up, which gave me time to finish the long checklist.

Les would fly this leg, giving me a chance to observe things and ask questions. One thing I needed help with was getting the air conditioning to behave. The thing would take forever to shift from full cold to the moderate air needed as we climbed, then warm air at altitude. Les had about five techniques to get the thing to behave. I was dumbfounded. In the 757, all I did was set the temperature and forget it.

The flight to Jacksonville was pretty short, and it seemed we had just leveled off before we were descending. I was very familiar with Jacksonville airport, as I had flown there for a regional airline a few years before. We landed and Les pulled us into the gate, with me scrambling to get the checklists done. I jumped out of the seat and went downstairs to do the walk-around, and by the time I got back upstairs, the new passengers were boarding already. I used the onboard lavatory and came out face-to-face with Jess. After looking at each other for a few seconds, we quickly shared our first flight experiences and then I had to get back to work. She did not blush this time. We would be leaving just as soon as the passengers were on board, to make up time and get back to the hub on time.

It was my turn to fly, and after Les lined me up with the runway, it was my controls, and I pushed the thrust levers forward, feeling the same thrill as always as the engines came up to speed and the acceleration pushed me in the back. The little airliner flew nicely, and I enjoyed the climb out and then engaged the autopilot so I could program the arrival. It seemed like all the planes that had left Atlanta earlier were back at the same time, and our arrival was so long, I was able to see the small airport where I used to flight instruct. Les grumbled about the long final approach. Eventually, air traffic control turned us toward the runway, and I clicked off the autopilot and hand-flew the jet to touchdown. It was kind of fun, and I was actually caught up enough to enjoy myself.

At the gate back in Atlanta, we were relieved that we were keeping the same jet for the flight to Buffalo. We had about 15 minutes to relax between flights. Les went up to the gate area to scrounge a newspaper, so I plopped down in a first-class seat to catch my breath. Nancy gave me another club soda, and we chatted about the layover.

Nancy said, "The hotel is pretty ordinary, but there is a nice restaurant within walking distance we can all go to if you want."

Jess had joined us from the back of the plane. I looked up at her.

"How does that sound, Jess? A crew dinner? We used to do that now and then at my last airline."

She blushed again. Maybe I embarrassed her. "That sounds good to me."

Les joined us and passed around the remnants of several newspapers. Nancy said. "We're all going to dinner together, Les. You're buying!"

Off to Buffalo

The gate agent came down and said he was ready to load, so we all took our positions. I had the flight deck ready in no time, and we pushed back on time and blasted off for the two-hour trip to New York. Les had me fly this leg for more experience, and I was glad to be getting the feel of the jet. It was a relaxing flight, and we started the descent on time. On the descent, I happened to glance at the engine gauges and noticed the right engine oil quantity was getting low. I looked at it again in a few minutes. Yep, definitely getting lower quickly. I pointed the problem out to Les, and we kept an eye on the quantity while on the approach. The right engine was losing oil, no doubt about it. We conferred, and since we were already on approach to Buffalo, we would continue. If it went below the minimum quantity during approach, we would shut down the engine and do a single-engine landing. Just like the simulator, I thought to myself.

We landed normally but shut down the right engine as soon as we could after the mandatory cooling time. We pulled into the gate, and I went down to do the walkaround required for an overnight, as this was our airplane for the morning. The right engine cowling was covered in oil, there was a leak in there somewhere. My aircraft mechanic background told me it was on the pressure side of the oil pump since we had lost so much oil so quickly. We called for maintenance, and they got a work stand and opened the cowling. It did not take long to find the culprit, a broken oil pressure sensor. Maintenance did not have one on hand, and they would coordinate with Atlanta to find out what to do.

We met the flight attendants at the hotel van waiting area. I stood next to Jess and engaged her in small talk. She was easy on the eyes and nice to talk with. We sat next to each other in the van, which was crowded as we had to share with a crew from another airline. It was close quarters, and Jess and I were close enough together that our hips were in contact, which I enjoyed. At the hotel, Les handed me my room key, and we all agreed to meet in an hour or so and walk to the restaurant. We rode up in the elevator together, with Les and I on the top floor, while the girls were one floor down. We said goodbye cheerily and said we would see them in the lobby in an hour.

I was in my room for about five minutes, just long enough to take my shoes and tie off after hitting the head when there was a knock on the door. It was Jess. She had changed to shorts and a nice tee shirt and had athletic shoes on. Our eyes met, and she asked if she could come in. I let her in and closed the door. When I turned to her, she put her arms around my neck and held me tight. I was speechless.

We stared into each other's eyes for a moment, then she said, "I've got to find something out." With that, she pulled me to her and kissed me with her mouth closed. It was a very nice kiss. She backed up and looked at me again, then came back for a full-up, no kidding, hello there deep kiss. Our tongues intertwined hungrily. I had my arms full of a warm, tall, good-looking, good-feeling woman who was intent on checking every inch of my mouth with her tongue. If this was the way all flights went, I was going to like this airline a lot.

After a while, she backed off, released my neck, and stood a foot away, smiling at me. "I thought so," she said.

I was feeling a lot of things going on in my body as if I had been struck by lightning. "And just what did you find out, Jess?"

"Whenever you looked at me, I had an overwhelming urge to kiss you and take you to bed. I had to find out if it was accurate."

"That explains the blushing. Was the feeling accurate?"

She nodded. "I don't blush. Yes, on the accurate. That was new to me, feeling flushed with excitement. What is it with you, Dirk? Do you always drive the girls crazy?"

I admitted that some women had a strong attraction to me. "I have no idea why. It just happens."

She put her arms around my waist. "Well, it's happening to this girl. Are you wearing that shirt tomorrow? If so, you had better hang it and your uniform pants up right now."

"Why is that?"

She sat on the bed and started taking her shoes off. "Because you have time to do me quickly before dinner, and I don't want to have to iron your shirt because we were rolling around on the bed with it on."

I smiled. "Oh, are we going to roll around on the bed?"

She grinned. "If you ever stop talking, we will."

A quickie

She pulled the bedspread back and pulled the sheets open as I was hanging up my uniform as fast as I ever had. She had her shoes off and was pulling her tee shirt off as I turned around. I noticed she had nice boobs, easy to see because there was no bra.

I said, "I can help you with the shorts."

She smiled, and said, "Come and get them."

I felt there was not enough time for anything fancy, so as she lifted her butt, I slid the shorts off, noticing there were no panties.

"You came prepared!"

She laughed. "I had a burst of self-confidence. If you had thrown me out, I would have to slink back to my room braless and with no panties. Shameless!"

Her pubic hair was nice looking. As a matter of fact, she was nice looking from the tips of her painted toes to her earrings. The boobs were a nice size, with cute pink nipples, now erect. Her body was slender, with no stretch marks and no scars that I could see. Her shoulders were very nice, and her stomach was flat. She had a great body. I was not exactly sure why it was lying naked in front of me.

I was pulling the rest of my underwear and socks off with her watching. She was on her back, waiting with a smile. I completed disrobing and lay down on top of her and kissed her. Our hands roamed each other, exploring. She had enough foreplay. "Come on, Dirk. I'm so hot I'm about to pop."

I reached down to her pussy and slid a finger between the lips. She wasn't exaggerating, she was wet and ready. She moaned a little as my finger went up and down the lips a little and then she moaned louder as I entered her vaginal vault. She reached down and grabbed my erect cock and pulled me to her. "Come on!" she whispered urgently.

I crouched between her legs and brought the head of my dick to her labia. She guided me to the right spot, and then surprised me.

She called out, "Wait!"

I did not push into her, although it was a powerful urge. "What?"

She looked at me. "You're not married, right?"

"I am confirming that I am not married."

She smiled. "Sorry! Forgot to ask. Go ahead!"

I had to laugh. I pushed in while I was still laughing, and she was, too. I took four or five short strokes to lubricate my dick in her wet pussy, then I was all the way in, enjoying the moment. Her pussy was tight, warm, and wet. It felt wonderful. She was impatient.

"Mmmmm. Come on!"

I started a nice thrusting rhythm and was very glad to see that she responded to each push with a thrust of her hips into me. There are so many women that just lay there. We had a nice motion going for a few minutes, then the urgency increased. Her breath became ragged and rapid, as her hands pulled me into her by the ass. She was ready to come any second, and I wasn't far behind her. I pushed into her harder and faster, kissing her deeply as I did so.

She cried out. "Oh, Dirk! That's it! Faster!"

I went into overdrive and was soon rewarded with a gentle scream of ecstasy.

"Oooooohhh! Ohhhhhh! That's it, that's it, oh, that's it! Ahhhhhhh!"

A wave of orgasm swept over her as her hips bucked into me and she pulled my face to hers for a big kiss. About that time, my balls exploded and I sent a load of hot cum deep within her. I slowed down, then stopped, holding pressure against her clit with my pelvis. She ran her hands over my back and ass, caressing me as she moaned and groaned. Then, as we regained our senses I rolled off her, and we turned to face each other.

She was smiling. "Yep! I was right about that feeling! I have never come that quickly!"

I smiled back at her. "I'd say we have an attraction of some kind."

"No kidding! I'd say our genitals are attracted; we'll have to find out about the rest of us." She looked at her watch. "I need to sneak back to my room and put on a bra, at least. Be a dear and grab me a washcloth out of the bathroom. I'll return one after dinner."

"After dinner?"

She grinned. "Yes, after dinner. That was just the warm-up, the quickie to get our heads clear. The main event will be tonight."

"I think you are forgetting this is a short layover and we both will need some rest."

"Hmmm. You may be right. We'll play that by ear later. I'll definitely be back, though. I'm not that easy to get rid of."

I handed her the washcloth and she headed for the bathroom with her shorts in hand. She came out a couple of minutes later, wearing the shorts and nothing else. She was beautiful. I admired her as she pulled the tee shirt on and shook her hair out.

"You're gorgeous, Jess."

She dimpled and bent down to kiss me. "That's just lust, my friend. Don't lay back down. You'll fall asleep and miss dinner."

"Yes, Ma'am. Are you always this bossy?"

She was smiling as she headed out the door. "I guess you are going to find out."

Dinner and Dessert

I went downstairs early and saw Les in the hotel bar, which was a surprise as this layover was short enough that it would not be legal according to company regulations to have any alcohol. He saw my face as I walked up and put me at ease. "I've been on the phone with maintenance control. They can't get a part up here to fix the jet until around noon on our next scheduled flight, and then they have to install the part and run the engine. Crew scheduling has reset our show time to 1300. We now have a long layover. Can I buy you a drink?"

"Yes, thanks. It'll be good to get more sleep." In my head, I was already thinking of Jess and a long night of passion. I could not help smiling.

We clinked glasses when my drink came. I thanked him for the drink.

Les smiled. "When you are a Captain, always buy drinks and dinner for your new hires."

It was my turn to smile. "I'll do that. When I was a regional Captain, I didn't have any money to do it then."

Les laughed, and about that time the three flight attendants found us and joined us. Les explained the situation and bought a round for everyone.

Jess had changed clothes into a nice blouse and the same shorts and athletic shoes. She had fixed her makeup and brushed her hair, and it was down now, not in the ponytail. She looked fresh and radiant. She looked at me and smiled without saying a word. I saw Nancy looking from me to Jess and back. I think she was getting an idea of how our last hour was spent.

Nancy smiled as she said, "How are our two new hires doing? Settling in?"

I said, "I'm still getting used to the jet. The airline operation is way different than at my last place, too."

Les chimed in. "He did great for his first day on the line. I can see his heavy jet experience coming out. We did well when we hired him."

It was my turn to blush. "Thanks, Les."

Les turned to Nancy. "And how did Miss Jessica do in the back?"

"Just fine. She is a natural people person; she can talk to anyone. Also, a good hire."

We finished our drinks and walked to the restaurant. It was a nice night, New York was nicer than Georgia this time of year. Jess walked with Les and the other flight attendant, while Nancy and I walked together behind them. She looked at me and quietly offered some advice, out of earshot of the others.

"Dirk, I've been around this airline a long time, and I'm going to say this not as a flight attendant supervisor but as a mentor. You and my young flight attendant both need to concentrate on getting through your initial operating experience and then keeping it together until you are off probation. Don't get distracted."

I looked at her. She was dead serious. "That's good advice for anyone, Nancy. Thanks. I won't screw this up."

She finally smiled and took my arm as we walked the rest of the way in silence.

At dinner, Les and Nancy entertained us with funny stories about their airline experiences. I was sitting next to Jess, but we did not get a chance to talk much. I was thinking about what Nancy had said.

After dinner, we walked back, this time with Jess and I together. I wanted to take her hand but knew that would not be appropriate. In the lobby, there was some fumbling as we all decided what to do. Les invited me for a nightcap, while the girls said goodnight and headed upstairs. Jess had whispered her room number to me before we parted company. I hoped the eagle-eyed Nancy had not noticed.

At the bar, Les was getting into storytelling mode, but I begged off after one drink and headed upstairs. When I got there, I called Jess' room. She said to stay put, she would be up soon. She was as good as her word, knocking softly after only a few minutes. As she entered the room and the door shut behind her, she turned to me and kissed me deeply as we put our arms around each other. She had changed back to the tee shirt, and I could tell from her chest against mine there was no bra.

Coming up for air, she said, "Nancy gave me a little briefing as we went upstairs that basically meant, don't fool around with the pilots while I am on probation."

I laughed. "I got the same briefing."

She looked at me with a devilish smile. "I interpret that as meaning you have to be done with me so I can get my FAA-mandated rest period. Let's see… 1300 show time minus eight hours is …"

I helped her out. "0500."

"Right! So I have to be in my room by 0500 to be legal."

She was a case. "Jess, there is a difference between legal and smart. We both need to get a good night's rest and not show up for work looking like we have been screwing all night, with sunken eyes and smiles of bliss on our faces."

She pretended to pout. "Okay, we'll have sex only once more, then call it an early night. But you have to make it up to me when we have days off back at the base."

I kissed her. "I promise."

"What do you want to do now?"

I pondered that. "How about we undress each other, get in the bed, and snuggle while we get to know each other."

She frowned. "Will there be sex somewhere in there with all this talking?"

"Yes, indeed."

"In that case, your plan is approved."

I laughed. "You have a military background."

She nodded. "Army, eight years as an emergency room medical technician. Got out as an E-6. I can tell you are military, too."

"Yep. Air Force. Aircraft mechanic for four years then cross-trained to the aircrew field as an air refueling operator. Twenty years, retired as an E-8. Senior Master Sergeant."

She smiled again. "In that case, I don't have to hold back my natural tendency to be a foul-mouthed Army wench. Are we ever going to fucking get undressed and get into bed? Damn!"

I could not help laughing. I reached for her tee shirt hem. "Hands up!" As she lifted her arms, I pulled the shirt off over her head. I was right, she was braless. I admired her boobs. "Nice rack!"

"See how comfortable we are with each other now that we have compared military backgrounds? Would you have used that terminology with a civilian girl?"

I thought briefly. "Probably not."

She nodded. "We speak the same language. Your turn." She pulled my polo shirt out of my shorts and kept going until it was off. "Now we fold our shirts, not throwing them on the floor like undisciplined civilians."

"Got it."

She folded both of our shirts and put them on the dresser. She then went down to her knees and unfastened my shorts, and worked them down my hips, taking the underwear with them. She joked, "Ooooh! Tighty whiteys! What fashion sense!"

I could not stop laughing.

She pulled the shorts and underwear down and I stepped out of them. She gave my bobbing cock a kiss while she was down there.

"Thanks!"

"Any time, Sarge." She stood up.

I did the same as she had, dropping to my knees and unfastening her shorts, and sliding them down her nice legs. There was no underwear. I gave her clit a kiss on the way down. She gave a little shudder.

"Don't start that shit, we still have to talk!"

This girl was keeping me in stitches.

She took our shorts, folded them, and placed them neatly on the dresser with our shirts. I led her to the bed, where we lay against each other and snuggled. I had my arm around her and was able to caress her back and ass while she alternated running her hand up and down my thigh and stroking my chest. It was very pleasant.

She asked, "Have you ever been married?"

Truthfully, I answered, "Yeah, once when I was young and dumb. It didn't work out."

She filled in the rest. "And full of come, right? Was it lust at first sight?"

"Yep. When the lust wore off, there wasn't anything left."

"Ouch. Does it still hurt?"

"No, it took a while, but I'm over it."

She smiled. "Because you have been banging flight attendants left and right, huh?"

I popped her on the ass. "No, you are my first."

"And hopefully the last. No, don't say anything, that was out of bounds."

I kissed her. "How about you? Ever been married?"

"It's kind of the same story. I thought I was madly in love with this civilian, so we got hitched, but it wore off and we just bitched at each other all the time. It was kind of embarrassing."

"Painful?"

"More ugly than painful, I'm glad we did not have any kids."

"Speaking of which, I did not ask you about birth control."

She rose up and looked at me seriously. "Dirk, I was hoping you had a vasectomy since you came inside me without asking. I'm fertile as shit! I may be pregnant!"

My face betrayed me. After a minute, she laughed uproariously.

"Got your ass! You should have seen your face! Yes, I am on birth control, you horny dork!"

I grabbed her and pulled her to me. "Why, you little ..."

She was still laughing. "Oh, Dirk! Your face. I'm sorry. FYI, have that discussion before you shoot a load of semen into the woman. I don't want you impregnating a generation of flight attendants."

"Noted." I was still embarrassed.

"Aw, I'm sorry. That was harsh. If I rub your dick will that make you feel better?"

"It would, but we may not be talking for long."

"Hmm. Not a problem. Would you like to rub my boobs that you have been staring at?"

"I would like that."

"Mmmm. That's nice. Do you have a free hand?"

"Why, yes, I do. Where would you like it?"

"Down here." She moved my hand to her pussy. "Since you shot a load of semen into me earlier, I guess giving me head is out of the question for tonight, eh?"

"I would request a cleaning of the playground first."

"Agreed. Would fingering that area gross you out considering any residual fluids?"

"Negative."

"Mmmm. I see you are proceeding on your own. Please continue."

We proceeded with foreplay, her stroking my dick and me playing with her boobs and gently fingering her slippery pussy. I put my finger into the vaginal vault and crooked it just so as Gabby had taught me so long ago, massaging the elusive G spot.

"Shit! That feels good! Damn! You are right on it! Ahhhhhh! Keep it up!"

Her pumping of my cock was getting faster and more intense. My dick was as hard as a rock by now. Her moaning and squirming increased. She wanted me in her.

"Shit! Dirk, get on me! Put it in me!"

"With pleasure!"

I crouched between her long legs and was at the labia within seconds. She reached down to pull me in quickly, and as wet as she was and considering the residual cum still in her, I slid right in all the way. She groaned loudly as I went in.

"Oh, yeah! That feels good! Oh! C'mon, Dirk! Fuck me!"

With encouragement like that, what's a guy to do? I cranked up the speed and intensity, and we enjoyed several minutes of nice humping, with both of us groaning and moaning as we enjoyed the pure pleasure of fucking. She was getting hotter and hotter, and I felt she would come again at any moment. I was playing with her boobs and squeezing the nipples, while she had ahold of my ass with one hand while hanging on to my neck with the other.

We were also getting hot physically with the effort, and sweat was forming on her upper lip and between her boobs. She called out, "Oh! Yeah! Yeah! Harder, Dirk! Finish me off!"

I went into hyperdrive and pounded away at her. I lifted her legs to my shoulders and drove it in even deeper. Her cries became more frequent and varied.

"Ahhhhh! Damn! Oh, shit, oh shit, oh shit! Oooohhhh! Yeah! Oh, there it is! Wow!"

She shuddered as the orgasm washed through her, and she grabbed my neck and smothered me in kisses. She encouraged me to come, which I was very close to.

"Come on, Dirk! Come inside me! Give it to me!"

I exploded into her, with jet after jet of hot cum splashing into her as I collapsed in a sweaty pile on top of her. She caressed my hair and back, kissing me tenderly all over my face, mouth, and neck.

After a bit, our breathing slowed and we looked at each other.

She was the first to speak. "Well! That was nice!"

"I must agree. I loved it!"

I rolled off her and we lay next to each other, caressing each other all over. I said, "I have to get you back to your room before lights out."

She laughed. "We are such a sticky, sweaty mess I think the cat would be out of the bag immediately."

"Hmmm. I could bathe you before you go. That way you would look clean and virginally pure if anyone saw you."

"Great idea. Let's hit the shower."

I love showering with women, I always have. My rules are, I wash your private parts, and you wash mine. She agreed with the ground rules and soon we were soaping each other and making sure the other was scrupulously clean. It was great fun, and although we had just had a very satisfying sex session, my cock was trying to wake up. It's all about being clean.

She laughed and said, "I appreciate the gesture, but I'm fucked out. I need you to put me to bed."

We dried off and decided what to do next.

"If we get back in bed and talk, we will probably fall asleep, then I'm screwed when I try to sneak back to my room," she said logically.

"Yeah, you're right. Let's get you dressed and back to your room."

She put the tee shirt and shorts back on, made easier by the lack of underwear. I put my undies back on and stood at the door with her. We kissed.

"See you tomorrow like nothing happened, Jess."

"Like nothing happened, you got it. In case we don't get a chance to talk tomorrow, you had better call me when we get back, or I'll hunt you down with a knife."

I kissed her again. "I'll see you as soon as I can."

She snuck out the door and I gently closed it behind her. I sat on the bed and thought for a while. My first day flying the line was very satisfying.

After a few minutes, the room phone rang. It was Jess. "I made it back to my room, and nobody saw me. Thanks for a fun first day on the line, Dirk."

"I was just thinking that very thing. Thanks for making it memorable, and to many more events similar to that."

"Goodnight, Dirk."

"Goodnight, Jess."

Back to Atlanta

We all met downstairs at the scheduled show time, with Jess and I sitting across the lobby from each other while we waited. We rode out to the airport, and each part of the crew busied themselves with their jobs. Les and I pulled up the weather and flight plans. The plane from Atlanta came in on time, and the needed part for our plane was soon in the hands of the maintenance techs. They installed the sensor, filled the engine with oil, did a test run of the engine, and pronounced it healthy. We loaded up with the passengers that were left and jetted off towards home.

Les wanted me to run the radios for the return to home base, and I did so, enjoying a pretty day. Nancy called up on the intercom and asked if we wanted coffee after she got done with serving First Class. We did, and a few minutes later, the door was signaled, and Jess came up with our drinks. That was a nice surprise. She said the service in the back was done quickly, and she had come up to help Nancy, thus getting the job of bringing our coffee. She had never been on the flight deck of an airliner, let alone in flight, so Les gave her a nice explanation of some of the basics. She admired the view out the front of the jet. As Les turned away towards his window for something, Jess was quick to put her hand on the back of my neck and gave it a quick squeeze, then left the flight deck. I felt warm all over for a while.

For once, there was little traffic, and we turned right into the west runways and landed. After pulling into the gate, a guy wearing a grey suit came onto the flight deck, said hello, and gave us a schedule change. Since we had missed our Jacksonville round trip, as a consolation prize we now had a Miami round trip, which we were legal for because of the late show time. We would have to bag drag to another concourse, which was the first of many in my career at the airline.

Les and I packed up and were getting ready to head out. We said goodbye to the girls. We all smiled at each other, and then they got busy with their packing. Nancy walked out onto the jet bridge with us and held my arm to stop me as Les started up the ramp. We were alone for a moment. She surprised me by leaning over and kissing me on the cheek. She smiled and said, "Take care of my flight attendant, Dirk. I don't want to hear that you did her wrong."

I looked her in the eyes. "I'll take good care of her." Then I followed Les up the ramp to the terminal.

I flew again that week, had some days off, and then finished my operating experience training on that trip. I was now legal to fly with regular Captains. The company kept me in Atlanta for another month, or the rest of a bid period which is how we got our schedules. After that, I would be going to the junior and least desirable pilot domicile in the company, which was New York City. For this month, the company paid for me to stay at a budget hotel called the Clarion near the airport.

Jess and I started a game of phone tag, not making contact for weeks. This was before the days of cell phones, and since I was basically a transient living in a hotel, I did not have an answering machine or way to get a message, other than Jess leaving a message with the desk. She was in an apartment with two roommates, and leaving a message with them was about the same as Jess leaving a message at the hotel. I had a pager at the time, so the company and Jess could leave a number. Finally, we got together on the phone and actually talked.

"Hey, Jess. It's good to hear your voice."

She sounded great. "Same here. I was thinking you had dumped me."

I was incredulous. "Dumped you? We haven't even started dating. How could I dump a girl I ..."

She laughed. "You're cute when you are flustered. When are we going to see each other?"

We compared schedules. We both had two days off later in the week.

"That sounds good, Dirk. Where shall we meet, I don't mean just for dinner. Are you at that hotel with every other new hire pilot in the company?"

It was my turn to laugh. "The Clarion on Virginia Avenue. Have you been here to visit other pilots?"

"No, but I've had several invitations. I know where Virginia Avenue is, off I-85, right?"

"That's right. To the west of I-85, across from the cemetery and next to the Waffle House and the barbeque joint."

"I'll find it. Plan for a few nights of passion together. Rest up."

"I'll do my best." We chatted for a few minutes, then rang off. I was smiling with anticipation at seeing her again.

My schedule had me flying the next day, this time with a new female Captain named Gina. We got along well, with a lot in common. She was an Air Force veteran like me but had been a pilot on KC-135s, which I had flown on as an aircrew member. Flying with male pilots, the talk during cruise flight was about cars, boats, motorcycles, planes, fishing, guns, or other guy stuff. I was learning that flying with females, we talked about relationships. Gina talked about her husband Matt and her kids. She then quizzed me about who I was seeing, so naturally, I talked about Jess.

Gina listened attentively and then had questions.

"So, basically after one night of unbridled passion, you are now excited about rekindling your romance in a dumpy hotel?"

I had given Gina the PG version of our short time together, but she was no dummy and put the pieces together. "Well, that's about it. I'm not sure what feelings I have towards her, I guess I'll find out."

She frowned. "Dirk, all you are going to find out by hanging the do not disturb sign out for a couple of days is that you enjoy sleeping together. When are you going to get to know her outside of the bedroom?"

She had a point. "I guess the answer is to get out of that environment and do other things."

"Or, just be together and do nothing. You should not have to entertain her."

I thought for a moment. "And, to complicate things, I am off to New York next month for who knows how long."

She sighed. "Dirk, I feel like your big sister telling you this, but be prepared for her to not follow you to New York, or to meet for a romantic getaway at any one of our hundreds of destinations. This brief period of lust may be all there is to it. Enjoy each other, have fun and a few laughs, but be ready for each of you to move on."

She had a good point. "Thanks for the advice, Sis."

Laughing, she said, "It's worth every penny that you paid for it. Now, if you could tear yourself away from the subject of romance, would you be so good as to check the weather in Dallas, which I believe is our destination?"

Passion at the Clarion

Jess showed up at the Clarion much earlier than I had expected on our first day off together. She called me from a house phone and got my room number. I offered to meet her in the lobby and walk up with her, but she refused and said she was on the way. I straightened up my room a little in the couple of minutes that I had. She knocked on the door and came into the room with her flight attendant roll-aboard suitcase.

She dropped the bag, put her arms around my neck, and kissed me thoroughly. "Mmmm. I have been wanting to do that for weeks! Why have you been hiding from me?"

I kissed her neck. "It's because you are so fat and ugly, I just don't want to be seen with you."

"I thought that was it." She looked around the room and walked over to look out the window. "Boy, the company spares no expense putting you boys up in this luxurious setting. There really is a cemetery across the street, I thought you were kidding."

"I'm very honest in describing the environment."

She came to me and put her hands on her hips. "I've been here a whole minute and you haven't started to undress me yet. Don't you like me anymore?"

"I adore you, but did not want you to think that sex is all I'm interested in."

She grinned. "That's all I'm interested in right now. This is the let's have lots of great sex part of our new relationship. We'll get to know each other later. I'm really turned on just being with you. What the hell is it about you?"

"You have fallen under the spell of my mystical power over certain women."

"It better be just this certain woman. Have you been banging any more helpless flight attendants since I've seen you?"

I laughed. "No, but is that relevant? Are we going steady?"

"Not technically. But, if I see you with another woman while I am in this state, I may just give you a vasectomy with a dull knife."

"Noted. For the record, I intend to date only you while we figure out what we are doing."

She smiled at me and put a hand behind my neck. She was tall and did not have to look up very much. Those pretty blue eyes were looking at me intently. "That, sir, is the correct response while I am this way. Are you done talking for a while?"

I showed her by pulling her shirt out of her shorts and began to lift it off her. She was wearing a brightly colored tank top over very short white shorts, accentuating her long, tanned legs. White shorts with tanned legs are a favorite of mine. I realized that she was not wearing a bra, which was a very sexy look. I confirmed this by pulling the top all the way off as she lifted her arms in cooperation. She stood before me, smiling as she reached for the top, and as expected, folded it neatly. Her bare boobs looked great, and I noticed she had a gold necklace on.

"Don't you have any undergarments, you poor girl? I'll take you to the thrift store if you need me to."

She laughed. "The tank top with no bra is for you, dork. Unfortunately, your fellow horny pilots hanging around the lobby swilling free coffee noticed my outfit as I jiggled past them. I'm afraid I have attracted unwanted attention."

"And you with your little suitcase, too. They probably thought you were a hooker."

"They probably were incapable of thought, while the blood was rushing to their penises."

"Most likely. Hold still, I'm going to take your shorts off now."

I got to my knees and unfastened the shorts, and with some difficulty due to their snug fit, started them down her firm thighs. I then took the shorts in my teeth and started working them down, kissing and caressing the inside of her thighs as I went. Getting down to the ankles, I removed them over her sandals, kissing her toes as I went. Handing her the shorts, I raised back up and kissed her on the labia through her cute black lacy panties. She made a sharp intake of her breath as I did so.

"Damn, Dirk! That is sexy as hell. Where did you learn to ... never mind."

I smiled. "A sexy Italian lady gave me lessons when I was an E-5."

"No shit? Give me her address, I'm sending her a thank you note! What else did she show you?"

"I'll demonstrate." I put her on the bed on her back after we pulled the bedspread back, then used my teeth again, and worked her panties down a little at a time. As I got the panties down to just above the knees, I went to her exposed pussy and first ran my fingers through the pubic hair and down the labia. Jess gave a little shudder as I did so and moaned. I admired the view for a moment. She had nice long lips on her outer labia, with a nice shield of flesh around the clitoris. The lips were just a little fleshy, and they looked inviting. I spread the lips with two fingers, and darted my tongue into the gap, touching only the pink flesh inside. I tickled the clit a little and made a brief exploration of the hole leading to her vaginal vault. She squirmed and moaned, and I could feel her trying to instinctively spread her legs, but they were constricted by the panties at her knees, which is what I had intended. She spoke up.

"Just FYI, you don't need to spend a lot of time on foreplay, I'm pretty worked up already!"

"Sorry, I want to demonstrate my oral skills, you're going to get the full treatment."

In a strained voice that was half moaning, she said, "That's not a bad thing. Press on."

I worked her panties down to her nice ankles and gently removed them. For some reason, she still had her sandals on, so I removed them, then kissed every one of her toes, and then the top and bottom of each foot. She was squirming and moaning as I did so. For a big finish, I decided to suck on the big toe of one foot. I'd never done that before, but it seemed like a good idea at the time. Her reaction was noteworthy.

"Oh! That is so fucking sexy! Damn!"

I worked my way back up her legs, kissing the inside of each ankle, shin, and thigh as I went northbound. As I got near her pussy, I was kissing the inside of her upper thighs when she grabbed my head with both hands and pulled it into her pussy, moaning and squirming continuously. I think she was ready for me to get busy with the oral program.

I buried my face in the wetness of her cunt and savored it. There is nothing like the smell of it, still fresh from her shower that morning yet with the slight anchovy-like aroma that is in every woman. I loved it. I put my tongue to work, first going up and down the inside of her lips. Then I stopped off at the clit and rolled my tongue into a straw shape and gently sucked the clit. Her hips about came off the sheets as she pushed her clit into me, and a loud groan erupted. Liked that, did she? I smiled.

Working my way south, I spread the lips again between my index and third fingers, and applied the middle finger to her hole, working it in and curving it to massage the G spot. Her moaning and squirming became more intense. I replaced the finger with my tongue, and pushed in as far as it would go, then curled it up and tickled. She about went crazy with that, so I kept that up for at least 30 seconds when she finally let go with a soft scream. Her orgasm was upon her, and she cried out in pleasure.

"Oh, oh, oh, oh! Ahhhhhhh! Damn! Ahhhhhhh! Oh, I'm coming, I'm coming, I'm coming, oh god, I'm coming!"

She bucked and moaned, pulled my face hard into her and groaned, then finally released my head and fell back on the sheets, sweaty and spent. Her breathing was rapid and ragged. I put my fingers softly against her clit and applied pressure to what I knew was tingling.

She reached down and held my fingers against her as her breathing slowed.

She raised her head with a smile. "Dang! You're pretty good at that! I've never come while getting head before. That was great!" Then she looked at me. "Dirk, you're still dressed! Damn, son! We need to get you naked and put you to work!" She sat up and started pulling my shirt and shorts off, this time not taking the time to fold anything. As I got naked, she sat up and put my cock in her mouth, and commenced a wonderful blow job. After a few minutes, she looked up, with some saliva drooling from the corner of her mouth.

"You're pretty hard. Do you want to screw me now or just have me blow you?"

"I am loving the blow job, but I'd like to get in you."

She sat up, wiping her mouth with the back of her hand. "How do you want me, sex fiend?"

"I think go onto your hands and knees. I like doggie style."

She started to roll over, then looked at me. "Just for clarification, we are talking vaginal sex here, right?"

"Right."

"Whew! Good. I thought I was about to lose my anal cherry there for a minute."

I smiled at her and patted her bare ass, now raised up to me. "Well, if you want to ..."

"Maybe later, wild man. This will be fine."

She wiggled back towards me, and I placed my cock at the door to her wet pussy, with her hand making sure I went into the correct hole. With my dick safely in the vagina, she braced herself. I took a minute to appreciate the view. She had a magnificent ass, with tan lines showing that she wore a skimpy bikini swimsuit. Her back was strong and straight, and her shoulders looked athletic. There was a faint tan line on her back.

I started stroking. "You have a fantastic ass."

She turned her head back towards me. "You are such a gentleman with your timely compliments. Nice rack, Jess. Nice ass, Jess. Did you think to comment on my hair or outfit? No."

It's hard to concentrate on stroking while laughing, but I tried hard. After a few minutes, it started feeling pretty good, so I cranked up the pace and went in a little harder. Within seconds, she said, "You can bang as hard as you want, Sarge. I'm pretty tough."

With that, I pushed in harder, deeper, and faster, increasing the great feeling and enjoying the fuck. I was going at her hard enough to generate the sexual flesh-on-flesh slapping sound that turned me on even more. She moaned a few times as I put the meat to her, and when I came with a loud groan, she let out a groan of her own in satisfaction. I stopped thrusting as my cock spurt into her, and she pushed back into me and wiggled her ass, which I enjoyed very much.

I pulled out after a minute and looked around for something to wipe with. I ended up climbing off the bed and heading to the bathroom to get a cloth, handing it to her as she lay in the same position, afraid to sit up as the sexual fluids would run out. She applied the cloth and headed off to the bathroom to clean up. Climbing back into bed, she said, "That was fun. When can we do it again?"

I looked at her. "That was very fun. I will need a rest break and likely a blood transfusion."

She looked at me incredulously. "Rest break? Jeez, how old are you, like 40?"

I glared at her. "42."

She laughed delightedly. "Oh my, are we sensitive about the age difference?"

I pulled her to me and swatted her bare ass. "Not at all. Well, maybe. How old are you?"

She smiled. "30."

I shook my head. "I'm robbing the cradle. You're 12 years younger than me? Amazing."

She curled up into me. "And you are ringing my bell more than any man ever has. Imagine what you were like in your prime!"

"I think that is both a thinly veiled compliment and an insult at the same time."

She looked up and kissed me. "You would be correct."

I sighed. "What am I going to do with you?"

"Right now, you can feed me. I'm starving!"

I was getting hungry, too. "What are you in the mood for?"

"Something quick and inexpensive. I'm on first-year pay, which sucks."

"Yeah, me too. I can't afford much until I get on second-year pay. How about the Waffle House next door?"

She grinned. "You really know how to wine and dine a girl, Sarge." She saw me looking at her. "Just teasing, that's fine. I like breakfast any time of day."

"Me, too. Let's get dressed."

Brunch and recreation

We got dressed and headed for the elevator. On the way down, I pulled her to me and kissed her. "I like to kiss in elevators."

She smiled at me. "It will be our tradition."

Walking through the lobby, some crews were waiting for the shuttle, some of which were in my new hire class. They said hi and watched appreciatively as Jess jiggled by. As we got outside, I said, "Nice outfit. It really compliments your nice ass and nice rack."

She shook her head. "That was lame, Sarge."

I took her hand as we walked down the block. She seemed to like it. We walked past the hotel pool on the way to the Waffle House. She said, "Want to go swimming later? Maybe have pool or hot tub sex?"

"Are you into public sex acts?"

"No, but you make me pretty damned horny. I'm trying to be helpful and come up with ideas."

"Really? You're still horny after that?"

"Yep. It's some kind of spell you have over me, like that Houdini dude."

"Svengali."

"Whatever. The point is that I'm turned on even after we did it and I had a wonderful orgasm."

I was shaking my head. "You are every man's dream. A beautiful nymphomaniac. If you owned a liquor store, you'd be perfect."

"Very funny."

We arrived at one of the South's more famous comfort food chains. We sat together in a booth. The waitress smiled at us; a couple obviously infatuated with each other. Jess ordered something reasonable, I was hungry and ordered like it.

After the waitress left, Jess said, "You ordered all that for yourself? You know I ordered, too, right?"

I was defensive. "I'm hungry. You worked me hard."

She put her hand on the waistline of my shorts. "Dude, you're 42. You can't eat like that anymore. You've got a cute little tummy roll going on here. Tell her to cut that order in half."

"Yeah, I guess you're right." I went and intercepted the waitress before she had called out the order to the cook.

Jess looked at me as I came back to the booth. "Are you mad at me for being bossy?"

I looked at her. "I think so, but I understand your point."

She ran her hand up and down my bare leg. It felt good. "You'll feel better after we have sex again."

"And when will that be?"

She smiled. "Obviously after lunch but before dinner."

"We can get a to-go bag."

"Don't tempt me, Sarge. I'm hanging on by a thread here."

We had lunch and strolled back to the room. Once there, we engaged in some kissing on the bed. There was nowhere else to sit. After a while, she raised up, and took off her tank top with one smooth motion, leaving her naked from the waist up. She folded the shirt, lay back on the bed, and looked at me invitingly.

I got the hint. My hands sought out her boobs, and while caressing them, we went back to kissing. That lasted several more minutes, and then she got up, stripped off her shorts and underwear, and climbed back in beside me. There was even more girl to caress and fondle while kissing, which was very pleasing. She rose up and regarded me.

"Dirk? Is there a reason you have all those clothes on?"

I couldn't think of one, so I stripped off as she watched me with a smile. Now we were both naked lying together, kissing and stroking one another. I played with everything in sight and then slipped a finger into her still-wet pussy. She groaned as I did so, and I tickled her G spot a little. That got her squirming again, with some soft moans. She had a fist around my dick, which had woken up and wanted to participate. After a minute or two of G spot tickling, she asked me rather breathlessly what we were going to do next.

"Let's put you on top."

She nodded in agreement, and I got on my back. She swung aboard, raising her ass up to get room to slide my dick in her. She slowly lowered herself, with a look of enjoyment on her face as she got it all the way in. She sat for a moment, getting used to the feeling, and smiling at me as she did so. It was very pleasant. She started a slow pumping and grinding motion, which got some moans out of her and some out of me, too. I knew she was enjoying it, but I wanted her to go crazy.

"Jess, push your hips forward and back, grinding your pelvis into me." She tried it and liked it, but it needed more mentoring. I put a fist in front of her pubic hair, resting against my belly. "Try and push my hand away. Use your clit to push against me like it's an eraser, and you are trying to get rid of my pubic hair."

She looked at me like I was nuts, then tried the motion as I suggested, with her eyes getting wider the more she ground her pelvis into mine. Her breath caught, and her eyes grew wild. "That's fantastic! That's just the right way to say that! Ahhhhhh! Damn! That feels good. Hang on, Dirk!"

She started rocking my world with the hip motion as hard as she could, with me pumping hard into her as she did so. Only a few minutes of moaning and intense activity later, she began to come again.

"Oh! Damn! Oh! Ahhhhh! Oh god, oh god, oh Dirk! I'm coming again!"

Her body shuddered and shook as the orgasm swept through her. She collapsed onto me as I pumped a few more times, then came. I groaned mightily as I shot hot cum into her. She lay on me, breathing hard. I caressed her sweaty back and ass, stroking her hair. After a few minutes, she rose and kissed me sweetly. She reached for a cloth next to the bed and rolled off me, still breathing hard as she wiped the juices off my legs and then put the cloth between her thighs. She rolled toward me and grinned.

"Don't tell me your sexy Italian friend taught you about that, too!"

"Truth. She would say things like, Dirk, tell your women to do this."

She looked me in the eyes. "You have to tell me more about this chick. Do you still see her?"

"No, I haven't seen her in a really long time, like 15 years. Last I heard, she was in Brazil or something."

"What was her name?"

I stroked Jess' hair. "Her name was Gabriella."

She kissed me and gently asked, "Did you love her?"

I thought for a moment. "I think I did. We had a hell of a summer, then drifted apart. It was probably better that way. Anyway, she was a hell of a mentor."

"And how old were you during this time?"

I laughed. "25. I was the absolute luckiest 25-year-old E-5 on the planet." I kissed Jess. "And now I am here with you, dear girl, and you are the object of my attention and affection."

She snuggled up to me. "Yes, you are here with me now. And I am grateful to Gabriella for loving you. I'm the recipient of that love, too." She rose up and looked at me. "Let's drink a toast to her tonight."

I smiled. "What a nice idea. She'd love that."

Jess lay back down, smiling. "Let's take a nap, Sarge."

My eyes were already closed.

Poolside talk

We napped for a while, then jointly decided we would go to the pool and swim a little and lay in the sun while planning our next move. She had a very skimpy bikini in her bag, and put on one of my tee shirts for a cover-up to go downstairs in. As we got in the elevator, she turned to me for her elevator kiss. It was a nice tradition. I admired her.

"My tee shirt has never looked so good."

"Better!"

"I'm trying."

At the pool, We lay in the sun on lounges next to each other for a while. She looked smoking hot in her bikini. I could not stop looking at her. She noticed, and peering at me over her sunglasses, asked, "Are you checking me out?"

"I am admiring your beautiful body and am very glad you have chosen to spend time with me."

She smiled. "Aww, that's nice. I'm enjoying our days off together."

"Jess, tell me about yourself. We've had sex together four or five times, had two meals together, and have not yet spent the night together, but I don't know anything about you except for the brief conversations we have had about our military backgrounds."

Nodding, she said, "That's fair. Okay, here goes. Army family, I was born in the Panama Canal Zone, we lived all over the place and were in a zillion different schools growing up all over the US and Europe. Dad retired as a 30-year Command Sergeant Major; they live in El Paso now. I've got three brothers, I'm the baby of the family. One brother went to West Point, he's still on active duty in the Army. The others are doing civilian things. I have six nieces and nephews, whom I adore. I went to college at a couple of different places, and graduated from UT El Paso, with a degree in business administration. I was thinking about going into nursing but decided to try the medical technician bit in the Army, liked that and did two hitches. Then I wanted to try something different, so after putzing around with a couple of business jobs, decided to be a flight attendant and see the world. I already told you about my brief marriage. I don't have any kids and don't think that's for me. Your turn."

I thought for a moment. "Okay. Grew up in suburban California, San Francisco Bay area. After high school, worked in a factory for a while, then joined the Air Force. Did a four-year tour as an aircraft mechanic and got both married and divorced during that period. Then cross-trained to aircrew, like I told you, doing a lot of instructing, then some staff jobs, finishing an E-8. Then after a career of that and doing flight training a little at a time, I went whole hog and came here to Atlanta to finish my training, then worked here for a couple of years building hours doing flight instructing. Got on with a regional carrier flying turboprops and worked my way up to check airman. Then I finished my four-year degree, and within a month I was at a major airline in Phoenix. I got about 500 hours in the 757, which triggered something at a couple of different big legacy airlines, and I interviewed at a few. Our airline offered me the job first, and I'd wanted to fly for them since I was a teenager so that was a no-brainer. No wives, no kids, no attachments. The only living member of my family left is my cousin, and we don't talk much. After this month, I'm assigned to New York."

She looked at me. "That's a hell of a path. Enlisted guy to an airline pilot. Have you ever thought about getting married again?"

I looked back at her. "Are you offering?"

Laughing, she said, "Hell no! I like being single. What about you?"

"I like it too. To answer your question, I'm not interested in any long-term relationship."

"Let's get in the water. I'm getting hot."

Splashing lazily in the water, she asked, "What do you do when you are not flying or chasing girls? Anything fun?"

"No, I live a pretty boring life."

"Have you had this experience with women wanting to screw your brains out before?"

"Yep. It just happens sometimes. Not real often."

She thought for a minute. "What happens when that wears off? Do they just say, 'Thanks Dirk,' and leave?"

I thought about my answer. "Some have confused lust for love and want to get serious even though I tell them up front that's not in the cards. That's what happened to me when I was young, and I ended up married. Others just quit calling back and I never see them again. Occasionally some will call when they get horny. Some want to come back for a while and resume things and date for a while, then they drift off again."

She swam over to me and put her arms around my neck, so I put my arms around her waist. Her pretty blue eyes were locked with mine. "What's going to happen with us, Dirk?"

I kissed her. "We will have a brief period of intense lust, then maybe you'll get your fill and move on. Or we may drift in and out of each other's lives when we need to. There are many possible outcomes."

She kissed me back. "Right now, I am in the lust phase, but I like the acting romantic part, too. I'm fine with all that, Dirk. It will play out over time."

"I knew there was a reason I liked you. You're pretty levelheaded."

She was grinning at me again, the serious stuff over for now. "You also like my rack and my ass."

"That, too. Along with your pretty blue eyes and fantastic body."

"Flattery will get you in bed with me, sir. Let's try the hot tub."

We climbed out of the pool and checked the temperature of the hot tub. She pronounced it satisfactory and got in while I hunted around for the timer. The jets came on with a low roar, and there were lots of bubbles.

We sat next to each other and enjoyed the hot stream of bubbly water in silence. Then she turned to me with a gleam in her eye.

I said, "Uh, oh! I can see the wheels turning in your head."

She laughed, and said, "Let's do it in the hot tub, Dirk!"

I looked around. "Are you insane? We're in public, with no shelter. Anyone could see us, especially from the rooms above us."

"Not if I sit on your lap facing you. People will just think we are kissing, which we will be. Here, like this." She got on my lap facing me. "See? You can't see through the bubbles at all."

"Aw, Jess. I don't know about this. We're on probation and in public."

"Where is your sense of adventure? She squirmed a bit. "Here, hold these." She handed me her swimsuit bottoms under the water.

"You're crazy!"

She put a hand on my rapidly swelling dick. "Been told that many times before. I prefer curiously eccentric. Hmm, he likes this kind of talk."

"This is very stimulating."

She put her arms around my neck. "Do you want to stick it up my ass?"

Astounded, I said, "I think I would prefer another venue for your first time up the ass."

She smiled. "He is getting really hard now. Go ahead and slide it in my pussy, then."

I pulled my dick up out of my suit and slid it in her, and it felt great. "Do we say pussy now?"

"Of course, I'm a foul-mouthed Army wench. Are you going to fuck me, or just sit there?"

"If I pump you, anyone will know what we are doing. I'll just try and wiggle a little."

"Mmmm. That's kind of nice. Here, let me squeeze it."

Her vagina contracted around my cock. "Wow, that feels great. Do it again."

She did. "How's that?"

"Fantastic! Are you sure nobody can see us?"

"Nobody can see us under the water. They'll just think I am getting you wound up for the bedroom. Let's kiss some more."

We did, and with me moving a little and her squeezing me, I was ready to pop after a few minutes. "Shit, Jess! I'm ready to come!"

She nibbled my ear lobe and whispered into it. "Please do."

I let loose with a torrent of cum, swirling into her amid the bubbling, hot water.

"Damn! That was great!"

She smiled, with her arms around my neck. "Glad I could show you something for a change." She slid off me and moved to put her knees on either side of a water jet, facing it. The bubbles were spraying straight at her pussy. "Mmm. This feels good and is rinsing me out, too!"

I shook my head. "Crazy."

We got our suits back on and climbed out just before the jets turned off. I hated to think what it would have looked like if they had shut off while we were fucking. That kind of risky behavior is not the way to act when on probation with a very conservative company.

We lay back on the lounges and sunned for a while holding hands. Clouds were rolling in, it looked like thunderstorms were on the way. After a few rumbles of thunder and some lightning, we went back to the room. We decided to take a shower to get the pool and hot tub water off us. A few minutes later, we were happily soaping each other under the warm water. I turned her away from me and spent a long time soaping her boobs and pussy, slipping a finger in her as she moaned. My cock was taking a break, but I offered to do her with my tongue and fingers.

"Let's just snuggle on the bed, Dirk."

We did while naked and resumed talking.

She was stroking my legs, stomach, and chest while chatting. "Now I can say I've done it with an E-8."

"I'm glad to be there for you."

She looked up at me. "What's the highest rank woman you've screwed?"

I looked a little uncomfortable. "Ahhh..."

She raised up with her eyes flashing. "Ha! Tell me! Come on! An officer?"

I nodded.

She would not let it go. "What rank? A Lieutenant, Captain? What?"

I winced and closed my eyes, embarrassed. "O-6."

She almost shouted. "A Colonel? A fucking full Colonel? Oh, Dirk! You HAVE to tell me about this. Were you still on active duty?"

"Well, this Army Colonel from FORSCOM here in Atlanta ..."

She was laughing. "An Army Colonel? Oh, man, that's even better! Tell me everything."

"She came to a lot of these airlift meetings that I went to, hundreds of guys attending, mostly Army. She was older than me, of course, but kind of pretty and really friendly, and I decided to see what I could do, so I started dogging her at every meeting. She started acting interested, so I turned on the charm, and one meeting, she asked me to come to her room after a social, and it just sort of happened."

"Were you an E-8 then?"

"No, I was an E-7. We did it, and the next morning went about our business as usual. Like nothing had happened."

She was entranced. "How was it?"

I raised up. "Why am I telling you all this? It's ancient history!"

She shook me by the shoulders. "Because I'm your friend and curious as hell about you. How was it?"

I shrugged. "It was okay, but not great. A few months later, I was in Atlanta seeing the FORSCOM guys and gave her a ring at her office. She said she would come to my hotel and have a drink after work. I was at the Marriott by the airport, nobody I knew was staying there. She came in uniform, straight from work, We had a drink, then she wanted to go to my room. There, she wanted it every which way, and I mean every way. She left about 0600 after we basically fucked all night. It was crazy."

Jess shook her head in fascination.

I added some details. "I remember doing her and glanced over to the desk chair, where she had hung her uniform shirt. I was banging away at her while looking at her rank insignia, the eagles, on her blouse. It was surreal."

Jess kissed me. "Sarge, you get around! What a story."

"Are you okay with that story?"

"Hell yes! That was in your past, and I asked." She kissed me. "It's totally fine. It makes me appreciate all you've done. Italian sex mentors, screwing the ass of an Army Colonel, what's next?"

I kissed her back. "Loving and appreciating a pretty lady named Jess."

She smiled and touched my cheek. "You're a nice man, Dirk Caldwell. We'd better get cleaned up for dinner. What's the dress code?"

"How about a bit more conservative than a tank top with no bra, but casual?"

"You got it. Let me fix my face and comb my hair and you can help me pick out what to wear."

Dinner with friends

I got dressed and turned on the TV to watch the local weather on WSB Channel 2. Thunderstorms and rain showers throughout the evening were on the forecast, and judging by the frequent booming of thunder were happening now. I called out to Jess.

"Jess, the weather is crappy. Why don't we just eat at the Mexican place downstairs?"

She appeared at the bathroom door in her panties and holding some girl stuff having to do with makeup. "Sounds fine."

"This comes with the warning that there will be a cohort of horny new hire pilots probably doing the same thing as us."

She paused. "So? Bra or no bra?"

"Yes, on the bra. We can't be responsible for new first officers falling over furniture and running into walls."

"Copy that."

She came out a bit later and put a bra on. She then gave me some options. I selected the navy blue miniskirt with a nice, collared blouse, and sandals. She put those on in front of me and came to demonstrate. The miniskirt made her legs look fantastic.

I admired her. "You are a picture of beauty, personified."

"And you are very sweet, but again full of lust."

We headed down to the restaurant. She said, "It's okay if some of your buddies want to join us."

"Thanks, Jess. I'm sure I will have more friends tonight than I ever have had before after they see you."

We checked in at the hostess stand and had to wait a few minutes for a table. As predicted, a couple of guys from my new hire class gravitated over.

"Hey, Dirk. You guys going to eat in? Mind if we join you?"

Why of course, you horny bastards. "Sure. This is my friend Jess, who is a flight attendant at our airline. Jess, this is Roger and Gene.

Being much more junior and less talented than me, they have been assigned as flight engineers on the 727 and banished to Miami."

Roger and Gene did not exactly trip over their tongues, but it was close. Jess was sweet to them, engaging them in small talk about where they were from, and that kind of thing. They were more or less at ease when we all got seated in a booth, with Jess and I on the same side. Jess and I ordered margaritas, the boys ordered a beer.

Our drinks came, and Jess reminded me, "We need to toast Gabriella."

"Thanks for reminding me, Jess." I raised my glass, and said, "To Gabriella, wherever she may be." Everyone said, "To Gabriella!" and clinked glasses or bottles as appropriate. I took my first sip of the margarita. It was very good.

Roger asked, "Who's Gabriella?"

Before I could think of an answer, Jess chimed in, "She was a mentor to Dirk when he was young."

Gene suggested, "Like an IP? Instructor Pilot?"

Jess nodded. "Something like that. She showed Dirk a lot. Right, Dirk?"

I nodded solemnly. "That's right. Things I am still using today."

The boys nodded their heads as if they understood.

Roger had another question. "Where did you guys meet?"

Jess was ready for that. "Dirk stood outside the flight attendant academy and handed out flyers with his contact information. I picked one up, and here I am."

They looked skeptical. We all looked at the menu. Jess looked at me and said, "Dirk, you don't need a full meal. These drinks have plenty of calories."

The guys looked at her in amazement. She clarified, "He's older, you know."

I stifled a chuckle. Gene asked, "Are you guys married?"

I finally got a word in. "No, but it feels like it sometimes." Jess smiled at me sweetly and reached for my hand under the table and put it on her bare leg.

The waiter came by for the food order. "Jess, may I order for you?" She nodded.

I said in Spanish, "¿Podemos la señorita y yo comer cuatro brochetas con bistec, pollo y camarones solamente, por favor?"

(Can the young lady and I have four skewers with steak, chicken, and shrimp only, please?)

He replied, "Ciertamente, señor. ¿Quieres tener arroz y frijoles?"

(Certainly, sir. Do you wish to have rice and beans?)

I said, "No, gracias. La chica piensa que ya estoy demasiado gordo."

(No, thank you. The girl thinks I am too fat already.)

He chuckled and turned to the guys to take their orders.

Jess asked, "What did you order us?"

"Some skewers. They'll be good. I told him you thought I was too fat, so skip the rice and beans."

She laughed. "Good choice. I didn't know you spoke Spanish, I thought you might know some Italian."

I said modestly, "I live in Phoenix, or did, I suppose. Spanish comes in handy out there."

Gene asked, "Where do you live, Dirk? I know you got tagged to go to New York, but where will home be?"

I thought for a minute. "I have all my stuff from Phoenix in my car. I still have a condo here that I rent out to some flight instructors, but they are going off to the regional airlines. I think I'll rent it out again, and just get something small in New York. I'd eventually like to come back here, but right now my bid is anywhere but New York."

Jess seemed interested in that but did not say anything. She chimed in, "My new hire flight attendant class is all Atlanta based. I guess they are building up the base for some expansion."

We talked about airline stuff for a while, and Jess asked the guys about their backgrounds. She had them identified before they could say a word.

"You guys are both prior military, right? What branch?"

They both admitted they were prior Air Force pilots. We all talked about our assignments in the military, and the guys were impressed with Jess' experience.

Our meals came, and Jess approved my lower-calorie version of the meal. I added, "That way we can get a second drink or dessert. What's your choice, Jess?"

"Dessert! But ..."

I jumped in. "We'll share dessert, right?" She nodded and smiled. I explained to the guys, "It's an Italian thing." They nodded but I could tell they had no clue what I was talking about.

Gene looked curious, and asked, "Didn't I see you guys in the hot tub this afternoon? I was looking out my window at the pool ..."

Jess and I traded glances. She said, "No, must have been someone else. Dirk's kept me captive in his room all day."

They both nodded. "Some guys are just lucky, I guess."

We finished the dessert, bid goodbye to the guys, and strolled towards the elevator. We had company in the elevator this time, but Jess turned to me and kissed me anyway, which made me warm all over. Our fellow elevator occupants smiled at the couple in love.

Back in the room, the same problem of where to sit occurred. I said, "Let's take off our clothes which now smell like Mexican food, and put tee shirts and undies on, so we can sit or lay on the bed."

Always thinking, Jess said, "Who needs tee shirts?"

"I like the way you think but was going to hold off on ravishing you until later."

She shrugged. "Tee shirts it is."

We dressed down, and propped up on the bed, close together. "That was a nice dinner. I can tell the guys liked you."

She smiled with no comment. Then she brought up a different subject.

"So, you need a renter for your condo?"

"Yep, just remembered that I need to be looking for some tenants."

She looked at me. "Dirk, rent it to me. My friend and I are looking for a place, we are sick of sharing with some of the other girls. We're both ex-military and probably better tenants than you could find. What would the rent be?"

I told her the rent I was getting for it and thought over the offer for a while. It was not as crazy as I first thought. Both girls had jobs, were probably more mature than most, and if her housekeeping habits were as I thought, would take good care of the place. I intended to come back and live in the condo someday and did not want to sell it.

"You know, that's not a bad idea."

She asked if we could go by and look at it tomorrow. I used the hotel phone and called the condo and got one of the guys and explained that I was bringing a woman by to look at the place. A woman. He got the idea. "We'll pick up a little bit. We're both working tomorrow during the day, so come by anytime."

It was a good time to just sit there and talk, so we did, about anything and everything. If the discussion had waned, I would have been tempted to turn on the TV, but we were engaged until Jess started yawning. She buried her face in my neck and in a muffled voice asked, "Do you want to have sex or go to sleep?"

"Since we only have had sex three times today, I will let you off the hook. Sleep is my vote."

"Sleep is agreed upon. Do you snore?"

"Not that I am aware of. You?"

"Same. Goodnight, Dirk."

"Goodnight, Jess. It's more fun saying it in person."

I could feel her smiling into my neck.

Sightseeing in Atlanta

I awoke and became aware that Jess was peeking outside through a crack in the draperies. "What kind of day do we have?"

She came and flopped down next to me. "Sunny and bright."

"Hmmm. Like you, my dear."

She smiled. "Go brush your teeth and we'll do our morning exercises."

I did and reported back to bed. She had shed the tee shirt and undies and was naked with the sheet pulled halfway over her. "My, don't you look sexy."

She grinned. "I've been awake for a long time but wanted you to sleep."

"You wore me out yesterday."

"I'm sure you will be okay. What shall we do now?"

I sat on the edge of the bed and pretended to think. "Hmmm, maybe we'll get coffee, then ..."

She interrupted me by pulling me into the bed and rolling on top of me. "Quit stalling! Kiss me and then show me more stuff!"

I kissed her and ran my hands over her bare boobs, then all over her. "Well, since you are already on top..."

"Yes? Get on with it, please!"

"First I want to see how horny you are." I slid a finger into her pussy, which was damp with excitement. "Damn, girl! What were you thinking about while waiting for me to wake up?"

She moaned a little, then grabbed my cock. "This!"

"I guess so, in that case ..." I pushed the finger in deeper and crooked it around to massage the G spot right away. She liked it.

"Oh! That's it! Ohhh! Dirk, can you please give me some head before we do whatever is on your plan? Please?"

"I can do that. Roll over."

She did and spread her legs seductively. I put my face right into her pussy and started up and down her slit, before sticking the tongue into the vaginal vault and curling it to the G spot. She squirmed and moaned. She was not kidding when she said she had been thinking about dick. I licked the G spot for a while, while her groaning and squirming increased. When she was good and ready, I pulled back, laid on my back, and had her get on top. She swung aboard, and quickly had my cock inside her moaning with the sensation.

"Now sit straight up, instead of leaning over bracing yourself on my shoulders like we did before." She did, starting the exquisite motion of clit rubbing. "Now sit up real straight, that will get you in deeper, the start that motion." She did, and her moaning said it was working for her. "This isn't a whole lot different, just some different feeling." She nodded and rode mc for a while, with her lower lip between her teeth, eyes closed.

"That's called cowgirl up like you are riding a horse. You can put your hands over your head if you want." She did and liked the feeling.

"I'm riding you!" she gasped out.

"Yes, you are. How does that feel?"

She nodded briskly. "Good!"

"Okay, now for something different. Climb off, then mount me facing away from me, then do the same thing."

She did and was soon mounted up facing away from me. "The feeling is still good, but I can't grind on you very well."

"Yep, but I can play with all your good parts." I demonstrated on her boobs, clit, and pussy.

"Mmmm. Yeah, I get that."

I wasn't done. "Go ahead and get off for a minute."

"Do I have to?"

I laughed. "You'll like this." I got up and got the desk chair and sat down on it. "Now sit down on me facing away again." She looked skeptical but did so.

"Now I have really good access to my favorite parts. I showed her by playing with her boobs, nipples, clit and pussy again.

She was moaning and squirming on me, impaled on my dick. "That's very nice!" she breathed.

We did that for a minute, and then I said, "Now turn around and sit on me with your legs outside mine." She turned around and slid in, and her eyes opened wide.

"Oh, Dirk! It's so deep! Damn! And all my weight is on my pussy! Oh, Shit!"

She started the clit rubbing motion as I pumped hard up into her as I was fondling her boobs. "Oh! This is the best! Damn! Oh, Oh, Oh, Oh god!" We could only keep that up for a minute or so.

She started trembling, then cut loose. "Ahhhhh! Damn! Oh! I'm coming! Holy crap! Ahhhhh!"

I pumped away into her and got caught up in the excitement and groaned loudly as I came in a jet of hot cum. "Damn, Jess! That was hot!"

She was still babbling. "Oh, my. Oh. Oh. Oh, my God!"

I stroked her hair and back as she slowly came out of her euphoric state. She had her head buried against my neck and was breathing heavily at first, now slowing down. She raised her head and looked me in the eyes, then kissed me gently.

I asked gently, "Are you okay, honey?"

She nodded her head, then spoke gently. "Oh, Dirk. That was amazing, but I think I'd better get off now."

The juices of our hot session were running out of her and across my thighs. She gingerly climbed off and headed for the bathroom. After a minute, she came out and handed me a cloth. I wiped down and went to lie back in bed while waiting for her. She came out and climbed in with me and hugged me tightly. She kissed me, and then, still clinging, described what it was like for her.

"That last part, the cowgirl on your lap was incredible. My weight was on my pussy, and my clit had so much pressure on it, I almost couldn't stand it. I kept grinding into you harder and harder, then it started to hurt a little. I couldn't stop, it felt so good and hurt at the same time. I think I'll be sore for a while, but that orgasm was worth it. It may have been the best one yet."

I stroked her hair. "I'm sorry you're sore. I was having so much fun seeing you worked up, I didn't realize it."

"It's totally on me. I was the one grinding away like I was pushing you through the chair. Was that more of the shit that Gabriella taught you?"

I nodded. "All part of my mentoring program."

She laughed. "You were the luckiest 25-year-old on the face of the earth to run into her."

"I was indeed. I think we need to get cleaned up and get something to eat when you are ready."

We cleaned up and went down to face the morning. The hotel had only pastries and cereal for their continental breakfast, so Jess nixed that, and we walked next door to the good old Waffle House for some protein. She convinced me to only have one sausage patty and some scrambled eggs. I normally eat a bigger breakfast than that, so this was going to take some getting used to. Over breakfast, we planned our day.

She asked, "Can we go see your condo first? I'm kind of excited by the idea. Then you can show me around Atlanta if you want."

"That's a good idea. I have a bunch of crap in my car I need to put into the storage closet there anyway."

We found my dirty car in the hotel parking lot and headed straight up I-85, through downtown. Traffic was pretty heavy, but we finally broke out, and since Jess was with me, I could use the HOV lane. Turning off at Indian Trail Road, we were soon at the condo. We both carried a box each to the door, and I let her in after knocking. My tenants were at work.

I let her in, then carried the boxes to the back door while she walked around, making approving sounds. I took her upstairs to show her the master and second bedrooms. She could not believe how nicely the place was furnished.

"Dirk, the furniture and wall art are amazing! Did a designer help you with this?"

I smiled. "A designer named Gabby. She got me a good deal on a bunch of Italian furniture from an importer and did the same with the wall art. I've had this stuff for almost 20 years."

She stared at me. "Gabby, like Gabriella? Man, she was so influential in your young adult life."

I nodded. "She really was."

We were standing in the master bedroom. She put her arms around me and hugged me tightly. "Dirk, will you rent this place to me?"

I kissed her gently. "I will as long as I can come to stay with you now and then."

"Deal! I'd offer to consummate the agreement with sex, but I might be too sore."

"I'm sorry, honey."

She smiled a shy smile. "That's the second time you've called me honey."

"I didn't know I was doing it. Is it all right?"

She kissed me long and deeply. "That signifies yes. Do you have a lease agreement and all that stuff? My friend and I need to give you a security deposit and all that."

I thought for a minute. "I have some of that paperwork in a file cabinet out in the storage room. Can you help me carry some more boxes up from the car?"

"Sure!"

We emptied my belongings out of the car and transferred them to the storage room outside the back door. In the room, I rummaged through some files and found a blank lease agreement.

"Here you go. We'll fill that out at the kitchen table and get copies at the Office Depot by the airport."

"I'll give you a check for the security deposit later, my checkbook is at my apartment."

I looked at her. "Security deposit? Aww, Jess, you don't have to."

She shook her head. "No, sir. This is going to be a business agreement like any other. Our relationship may go to shit, and you could be stuck. I want it this way."

I shrugged. "You're right."

I showed her around a little more, and she had good questions. Who are the utility companies, where does the trash go, where are the mailboxes, and what is the parking situation? All good questions. We were getting ready to leave, but she wanted to sit on the couch and kiss for a while. I didn't mind that at all. After a few minutes, she pulled back and looked at me.

"So, that's your bed in the master bedroom, right?"

"Yes, Ma'am."

She smiled. "How about this? I promise never to have sex in your bed except with you for the duration of the lease."

"I'll add that as a condition. Agreed. But why? If you rent the place, you can sleep with whomever you please."

"I know, but I want us to be exclusive for a while until we decide where this budding love affair is going."

I kissed her. "I'll agree to that also."

"So, no banging flight attendants until I advise you that you are released. Agreed?"

"How about non-flight attendants?"

She punched my shoulder. "You are such a pig! No banging anyone else, is that clear?"

"I agree. Do we have a budding love affair?"

She put her hand on my cheek and looked into my eyes with her lovely blue ones. "To be honest, I don't know. As we talked about, lust is running rampant right now. Let's wait and see."

We locked up and left. I wanted to show her where the MARTA train station was, so we went back that way. I pointed out the business airport where I used to flight instruct near the train station. She wanted to go by the old flight school, so I drove over there. Once there, she wanted to go in and look around. I had not been there for over a year and would like to see the owners again, so I agreed.

We walked into the place and were greeted by the owner, who was astounded to see me. After chatting for a while, I showed Jess around, even walking around the flight line and showing her the very airplanes I used to instruct in. She was fascinated, having never been around small single-engine planes before. We ended our tour of the airport by dining on small chili dogs at the Krystal drive-in on Buford Highway. It brought back fond memories.

Since we were out that way, I drove us over to Stone Mountain, and we looked in awe at the carving of Confederate Generals on the side of the huge hill of granite. After that, she was done sightseeing and was ready for some pool time, so we headed back to the hotel.

She announced, "After some pool time and maybe a nap, let's go over to my apartment and I'll get you that check for the security deposit."

"You can just mail it to me, once I get a mailing address in New York."

"Are you sure? We had a hell of a time getting ahold of each other for this extended date."

"I've about decided to get one of those new cellular phones, so we don't have to go through that again. It's about the same as paying for hotel phone calls. Then I'll have voice mail and messaging."

"Hmmm. Maybe I'll get one, too. Knowing you, you've done exhaustive research on plans and costs and all that shit."

I had to laugh. "You are beginning to get to know me. There is a store near here that has the carrier I'm going to use. We can go after swimming, and you can check them out."

Back in the room, we changed into our swimsuits and lay on the bed kissing and stroking for a while. I had to go get in some cold water after that. As we lounged in the pool, chatting about this and that, I began to wonder if this was going to end well. Would we be happy with occasional sex visits, or would there be more? Time will tell.

New York then back to Atlanta

I finished my month in Atlanta and drove my old car north up I-85 and I-95 to the greater New York area. My advice is to avoid going through the Washington, DC area. It's worse than Atlanta for traffic. After checking in with the airline at LaGuardia airport, they assigned me an airport hotel for five days until I found a place to live. There were a lot of crash pads with 6 or more pilots assigned to one place, and I signed up for one that had convenient public transit to the airport. It wasn't expensive but it was crowded and noisy, making me miss even the tiny apartment I had in Phoenix. I would be flying as much as I could, so it didn't matter to me.

Jess and her friend moved into my condo while I was in New York, and we communicated every few days on our new cell phones. We enjoyed talking about most things and managed not to talk about our relationship. Jess asked me when I would get a string of days off, and after comparing schedules we found a compatible date in a few weeks, and she asked me to come to stay with her. That sounded like fun, so I rode our airline down to Atlanta and she met me at the MARTA station in Chamblee.

She ran to me and greeted me with a big hug and a sloppy kiss, and I was very happy to have my arms wrapped around a tall, pretty girl. "I've missed you, you big dork!"

I looked into her blue eyes and big smile and felt myself falling into that loving feeling. I had better shake that off. "To think I flew a thousand miles to be called that. There's gratitude for you!"

She laughed delightedly and held my free hand as we walked to her car. "To show my gratitude and undying appreciation for you letting me rent your condo, I shall cook for you!"

"That sounds nice. I didn't know you had domestic skills."

"You mean besides in the bedroom, I assume."

There was no good answer to that. "It's really cooled off since I left."

It felt good to be in my condo after so long. I took my suitcase upstairs and changed clothes while Jess puttered around the kitchen, humming to herself. When I came back down, she had made us drinks, and we sat around the kitchen table visiting. She kept smiling and smiling, happy as a clam. There were some healthy snacks she had made, and I managed to choke those down.

I said, "You are a poster child of cheerfulness and radiating happiness."

She laughed, "I can't help it! I'm so happy to see you!"

I took her hand. "I've missed you, Jessica."

She almost shuddered. "Wow! When you said my full name like that, I got goosebumps. What the hell is that about?"

"We are enjoying the euphoric reunion feeling. By tomorrow, you'll be saying to yourself, 'When is that asshole leaving?'"

"Well, maybe not tomorrow."

"You know what I mean."

She looked into my eyes. "I'm enjoying this romantic part. If it lasts, that would be great."

"I like it, too."

She stood up. "Shall we have reunion sex now or after dinner?"

"Why can't we do both?"

She grinned. "I like the way you think, Sarge." She turned to the stove and turned the burners off. "To the bedroom!"

"The couch is closer."

"I'm not going to risk staining your nice furniture. Come on!"

I enjoyed walking up the stairs behind her. She really did have a nice ass. We got to the bedroom and started ripping the clothes off each other, with her interrupting each phase to neatly fold the clothing item that had been removed. Soon, we stood together naked, except for her necklace. I always enjoyed that touch. We ran our hands all over each other as we kissed passionately. I warned her, "This one is going to happen quickly. My libido is on max overdrive."

She was dragging me over to the bed. "Just give me some head, then you can fuck me! I've been going crazy thinking about it!"

We managed to pull the bedspread off and were lying on the sheets. I had her scoot to the edge of the bed, on her back with her legs hanging over the side. I knelt on the floor and spread her legs wide and pulled her ass to the edge of the bed. I was looking at her beautiful pussy, admiring the shape of the labia, and the clit at the edge of the nice furry mound. I ran a finger up and down the lips and tickled her clit. She gasped. I then spread the lips with two fingers and made an exploratory inquiry with the tip of my tongue. A nice moan was heard.

I worked up and down the inside of the lips, giving her clit some attention with my tongue curled like a straw. She groaned and squirmed. Back down the slit slowly, I worked to her hole and pushed my tongue in slowly, then wiggled it back and forth. She put her hands on my head and pulled me deeper into her pussy. I smiled. She wanted me to massage her G spot with my tongue. I was going to make her wait a little bit longer. I left the hole and worked up and down the labia a few times, giving the clit some love on each trip north. Her moaning and squirming were constant now. I decided to give her what she wanted, and went deep into the hole, curling my tongue upward. She drew a sharp breath and gasped.

"Oh, that's so good! So fucking good! Mmmmm."

Her fingers were running back and forth through my hair now, and I was able to reach up and fondle a boob and squeeze the nipple while tonguing her. It's good to have long arms. She liked that and was ready for some dick.

"Get on me, Dirk! Give it to me!"

Encouraged, I left my pussy licking post, stood up, took her hips in my hands, and pushed my cock directly into her wet pussy with her on the edge of the bed. She was surprised by the passion of that and reacted immediately. "Oh, oh, oh! That's what I've been wanting. Oh, Dirk!"

We were both pretty fired up, and after only a few minutes of frenzied thrusting, moaning, and groaning, I came in a rush, and she joined me. We both groaned loudly as I pushed deep into her and shot load after load of cum into her throbbing cunt. We stopped moving, and I realized she had her hands on my ass, pulling me into her. I raised a little and used both hands to caress her boobs, then leaned down to kiss her tenderly. She caressed my chest and waist while we were joined together by my shrinking cock.

After a nice moment, she smiled at me. "I think I missed you!"

"And I missed you, honey."

She dimpled. "I just love it when you call me that!"

I smiled. "I can say sweet things in Italian, too."

She laughed. "I bet you can. Say something, and I'll see if I like it."

"Jessica, mio caro."

"Oh, that's sexy. What does it mean?"

"It means my darling. Then there is amore mio."

"Nice. Amore is love, right? My love?"

"You got it."

"I like them both. Feel free to use them in your normal sweet talk after sex. Or during. Or before! Or while we are walking, holding hands."

"Certo, amore mio."

"Now you're just showing off. I like it, though. Let's get up so I can feed you."

We cleaned up and enjoyed a great meal. After, I helped her clean the kitchen, and we got a drink, then went to sit on the couch. I put on some nice, soft music. My couch, with a tall, pretty girl, who was just flushed enough after sex to look radiant. It was very nice.

I asked, "How are things here in Atlanta? I forgot to ask, where is your roommate?"

"Things are good. I get called out to fly pretty often, usually for out-and-back trips the senior girls don't want. I like using the MARTA to get to the airport, you were right, it's so much less hassle than driving all the way to the employee parking lot. My roommate Sandy is on a two-day trip, she'll be back tomorrow. She knows you will be here and wants to meet you."

"I'll be glad to meet her."

"Oh, you have some mail. I put it on your desk. I got you an inbox to keep things tidy."

I had to smile. "Of course, you got an inbox. You are keeping me organized, and I appreciate it."

She frowned a little. "I hope you don't mind, I looked at the return addresses to see if you wanted me to open them or not. A couple looked like bills and some advertisements like pre-approved credit cards and stuff."

I thought for a minute. "If you don't mind, please open what you think you needs attention and toss out the rest. I may leave some checks here for you to pay a bill if it is due soon before I get back here. Just let me know the check number and amount. Would you mind doing that?"

She smiled. "You must trust me a lot. That makes me feel good all over. Of course, I'll do that for you. It's part of the girlfriend package."

I already had my arm around her shoulders, so I pulled her close and kissed her long and lovingly, then looked into those pretty blue eyes. "I trust you with my heart and my checkbook, mio caro."

"Now that made me feel tingly. You are a smooth talker, Sarge. Have you been banging any of my fellow flight attendants while you have been in New York?"

"Flight attendants? No."

She laughed. "I can tell by how horny you were that you have been abiding by our agreement to be exclusive."

"I have. I don't want to screw this up in case you decide to keep me."

She touched my cheek. "I'll let you know."

We talked comfortably for an hour or so, then we both started yawning. We closed down the lower floor and went back up to the bedroom. There, we made slow, sleepy love for a while and both had a nice but quiet orgasm. We snuggled close together, talking softly. I was in my own house with a beautiful girl, in my own bed. I fell asleep smiling.

The next day was comfortable and quiet. I paid my bills, checked my schedule on the computer, and we walked to the nearby grocery store together, and then both of us sat on the couch reading. Her roommate came in before dinner, and we all had a nice visit before sharing a meal. After, we all cleaned up, then went to the small living room and chatted for a while, then turned on the TV. They picked out some romantic comedy to watch, and I didn't care. It was very relaxing and nice. That night, Sandy said goodnight early and went on up to her room. We went up later and made out quietly enough that Sandy may or may not have heard us.

After a few pleasant days off, I had to get back to New York. Both the girls drove me to the MARTA station, and Sandy sat in the car and tried not to look as we kissed goodbye. I didn't care if she watched. As I sat on the train and watched Atlanta slide by out the windows, I felt good about the visit. We had been romantic, domestic, and sexy. I was enamored with Jess, and I could tell she had strong feelings for me. Where would we be in a month? Six months? A year, even? I sighed and pulled out my airline timetable to look for a flight back to NYC and the dreaded crash pad.

A year goes by and a good deal occurs

Time passed. I got off probation, got a very nice pay raise to the second-year rate, and was very comfortable with flying the MD-80. I spent the next year doing the same type of visiting with Jess. We would compare schedules and find a period of days off to see each other. The reunions were always happy and romantic. While it was not routine, it was similar enough to a married commuting lifestyle to be scary. We stayed exclusive to each other, even though I had several offers, not all from flight attendants.

My airline started taking deliveries of the new Boeing 777 airplanes, which caused a surge of senior pilots bidding for that airplane from other fleets, causing vacancies in prime locations. I was able to get a bid for my airplane in Atlanta, which led to a problem, which was both good news and bad news. Would I toss Jess out of my condo, or move in with her? Both options were fraught with consequences. I decided to tell her face-to-face rather than over the phone. We had a visit coming up the next week, it could wait until then.

The first night of that visit, we were cuddled up on the couch, with the TV on. I decided it was time to talk. "Jess, I have something important to talk about."

She immediately turned the TV off and half turned to focus those blue eyes on me. "What's up?"

"I got a bid award to come back to Atlanta on the MD-80, effective next bid."

She brightened up. "Oh! That's great! That means you will be ..." She stopped, a frown overtaking her face as she realized what that meant.

"That's right. We have to decide if I will be living here with you or living separately."

She nodded. "I can see why you have been quiet since you got home. This is a major decision for us."

"That's what I was thinking. We have to approach this carefully."

She scooched up into me. "Part of me says I want you here with me all the time."

"Me, too. What's the other part saying?"

She wasn't falling for that. "You first."

I took a deep breath. "My other part is saying that living together is too much of a relationship commitment."

I could feel her nodding into my neck. "If you still made me pay rent, then you would just be sleeping with your tenant."

That made me chuckle. "I'm sure I can arrange a discount for services rendered."

It was her turn to chuckle. "Yeah, like 50 bucks off for each blowjob rendered during the month."

"50 bucks!"

"Aren't they worth that much? Hmmph. See if I ever do that again."

We sat together in silence for a couple of minutes, with me stroking her hair. I finally asked, "What do you want to do, amore mio?"

She sighed. "How about we try living together for a while? If we can do that without killing each other, that's saying something. I don't want to get married, and I'm sure you don't want to either. We're stuck in this weird middle territory."

I nodded. "I like that answer. Let's give it a try and see what happens. We'll know after a while. We've come a long way in the year and a half or so since we met."

"Yes, we have." She pulled back a little and locked eyes. "I love you, Dirk. But I don't want to screw up what we have by getting married."

My lump rose into my throat, and I choked up. "I love you too, Jessica."

She smiled sweetly, and put her hands on each of my cheeks, then kissed me very tenderly. "I've been aching to hear you say that, amore mio. You may say it as often as you wish without fear of marital entanglement."

"I may just do that. That was a great use of Italian, by the way."

"Thanks. It just flows, doesn't it?" She looked at me again. "Are you still going to charge me rent?"

"Damned right I am."

She shook her head, then leaned into me. "Asshole landlord."

At the start of the new bid, the company gave me a few days off to move, and I packed my crap back into the car and was ready to head back down I-95. Jess had days off and wanted to drive back with me, so she flew up to NYC and joined me. We enjoyed a leisurely drive back, stopping in DC to see some sights.

Soon, we pulled into the condo and Jess and Sandy helped me carry boxes in. We all looked at one another, knowing the dynamic was different. Sandy went upstairs and left Jess and me alone. It was a little awkward, knowing I was there to stay. I had to say something.

"This feels different already. Kind of weird."

She nodded. "I feel it, too. It's okay, just different. Like that commitment thing we have been avoiding."

I agreed. "It's like we have changed the relationship to a new level. Like we have to make it work, or else."

She shook her head. "That's too heavy for right now. Let's get you unpacked. I cleared out some room for you in the dresser and closet."

It made me smile. "We'll be sharing a dresser, how romantic."

That got an eye roll out of her. "Oh, yeah. Soon we will have more long, romantic discussions about where to hang our towels and put our toothbrushes."

I pulled her to me and planted a big kiss on her, and the serious mood lifted. "Lead on. I like to watch your ass as you go up the stairs."

She smiled, "Whoever said you weren't a romantic, Sarge?"

As we walked up the stairs, she gave her butt a few extra exaggerated wiggles for me, looking over her shoulder and grinning. What a girl.

A new airplane and the mood changes

As part of the migration of senior first officers to the new, shiny 777 airplanes, openings in previously very senior fleets were opening up. I was awarded a bid on the Boeing 767 in the international division, which meant I would fly both it and my beloved 757 across the ocean. My goal of being an international airline pilot was getting closer, and I was on cloud nine with happiness, and eagerly awaited the school date for training. Jess shared my enthusiasm, and we celebrated my good fortune with a dinner out at a nice Atlanta restaurant called Joey D's. We shared some wine and had a great dinner, with me excitedly describing the features of the 767 while Jess smiled and listened patiently. We decided on dessert and coffee at a nearby Denny's restaurant to save a few bucks. Of course, we shared the dessert.

Once back home at the condo, I was still hyped up and we enjoyed a fairly active and noisy sex session. Sandy was on a trip, so Jess could be as vocal as she wanted as I gave her a great tongue session and an enthusiastic fuck. As she achieved her climax, she almost shouted.

"Aww, shit! Oh, damn! Oh, oh, oh, oh, God! Ahhhh! Oh, Dirk! Oh, wow!"

I finished as well, and we clung together, breathing heavily. She looked at me and grinned. "I love Sandy like a sister, but I really enjoy sex more when she is on a trip!"

"I think you liked that."

She smiled and caressed my hair. "I did, and you did, too, Sarge. We have been getting a little routine in our lovemaking here in the past few months. It's good to cut loose now and then."

"I agree that you should put out more."

She punched me in the shoulder and glared at me. "You get it more than any of your horny pilot buddies, and you know it!"

"I admit that I am very lucky to have a beautiful, youthful, energetic, and loving sex partner who gives it up more than most other women."

She was mollified. "That's more like it. Rest up, and you can have it again in the middle of the night."

"Have I told you today that I love you, Mio caro?"

She smiled. "Keep that up, and you may get it again right now."

I underwent the very thorough 767 ground school and simulator training and after months of training was out on the line flying several trips domestically before they would take the training wheels off and let me fly over an ocean. That day came, and I flew with a wonderful check airman to London Heathrow in the UK, had a long layover, then headed back. It was great fun, and I was reminded of my Air Force days flying over the water in a tanker, only this time I was the pilot. I felt a great deal of satisfaction.

Some months passed, and I was beginning to feel a bit of change in Jess. It seemed like she was moody about something but would not talk about it. Then one night it came to a head. She came home from a trip that was full of crappy passengers, delays, airplane swaps, asshole pilots, shitty gate agents, and about everything else that could make a person grumpy. Sandy and I were at the kitchen table, drinking wine, eating brownies that Sandy had made, and playing cards. Oh, yeah it was raining like hell. She came in, dripping, her hair a mess, and with a look in her eye that would cause a sane man to run for cover. She started in a bitter tone, "Well, don't you two look cozy and warm drinking wine, a perfect couple."

Sandy and I looked at each other, we had not seen this side of Jess before. I offered her a glass of wine. "I'll get it myself!" Okay, then. We made room for her at the table and asked about her trip. She sat down in her uniform and started a good rant, It's good to get it all out, and Sandy and I listened sympathetically as she ran down the list of disasters and crappy people she had endured for the past three days. She gulped down a large glass of wine and poured another, then not long after that, another.

Calming down a little, she helped herself to a brownie and we dealt her into the card game. After a half hour or so, she drained her glass and went to pour another, that was her third large glass of wine, more than she usually drank. The bottle was almost empty. "Dirk, can you open another bottle?" I hesitated, thinking she may have had enough when she said, "Fuck it! If you aren't going to do it, I will!" and proceeded to open another bottle, a little shaky on her feet. She topped up her glass and offered the bottle to Sandy and me. "C'mon, have a drink with me. My best friend and my boyfriend! My two best friends!"

We each poured a little into our glasses, and after a few minutes of semi-drunken conversation, Sandy got up to leave saying she had a trip at midday and needed to get some sleep. Jess said, "Wait a minute! I want you here when I ask Dirk something."

Sandy sat back down. "Okay, Jess. I'll stay a minute."

Jess wobbled a bit, then said, "Okay! Here it is! Dirk, how come you're here with me? This is all fucking and no real relationship shit going on here! All you want to do is fuck me! How come you get to fuck everything with a skirt, and I am faithful to you? What is it with you and my best friend Sandy here? How long have you been fucking her behind my back, huh?"

We were shocked. I spoke up angrily. "Jess, you know good and god damned well that I have not touched another woman since we met! And that accusation about Sandy is just wrong! We're friends because of you, damn it! What the fuck do you think we should do when you aren't here, lock ourselves in our rooms?"

Sandy was crying. "Oh, Jess! You've got it all wrong! There's nothing between Dirk and me! What's gotten into you?"

Jess was on a drunken roll. "I expect you both to deny that shit! And another thing! Dirk here said he would fuck me up the ass and hasn't yet! When are you going to do that, asshole? How about tonight? Or you can fuck Sandy up the ass and then me! How about that?"

I had about enough. Angrily, I said, "Jess, I have had enough of this crap! I don't know where it started, but it ends now!"

She leered at me drunkenly. "Or what, big man? Or what? We ain't fucking married! You can't fucking order me around! Fuck you!"

I stood up. "Okay, Jess. That's enough. I'm going upstairs, you can join me when you calm down. Or not, that's your choice."

Sandy, still crying, joined me in heading upstairs. I heard Jess yell out as we started upstairs, "That's right! Have her walk up the stairs first so you can watch her ass wiggle!"

At the second-floor landing, Sandy and I looked at each other. I was shaking with anger, and Sandy's chest was heaving with sobs. We could hear Jess yelling at nobody down in the kitchen. "Dirk, I've never seen her like this. What shall we do?"

I shook my head. "I don't know what's wrong. I'll try and find out when she calms down, probably in the morning."

Still shaking with anger and disappointment, I dressed for bed and lay there stewing for an hour, my mind racing. The noise had stopped downstairs, and I went back down to check on Jess. She was sprawled out on the couch, passed out. She had spilled a glass of wine on the couch that Gabby had helped me buy. I shook my head in disgust. I mopped up as much of the wine as I could, took her uniform jacket off before it got ruined, and hung it in the hall closet. I put her legs up and turned her head sideways, so if she vomited at least she would not aspirate any. With a final look at her, I felt a moment of compassion and found a small blanket to throw over her. I loved her and wondered what the hell had happened to make her snap like that.

Sometime in the early morning, I heard banging and thumping. I got up and looked down the stairs. Jess was trying to come upstairs but couldn't make it. I did not want her to fall, so I went down and tried to help her walk up, but that was not working, so I took her down to ground level, and in a fireman's carry, tossed her over my shoulder and with some effort, carried her up the stairs. Sandy was watching from her door, with a frightened look on her face. "Is she all right?"

I answered grimly. "She's a drunken mess right now. I'm going to get this uniform off her and put her in bed."

Sandy asked, "Do you want some help?"

Jess was like a rag doll. "Yes, please. She's absolutely limp and hard to handle."

I carried Jess into the room and rolled her into bed. Between Sandy and I, we got her undressed down to her underwear, then I found an old tee shirt to put on her. I didn't want her to throw up on anything nice. We pushed her into bed on her side, and I put a waste basket near her head in case it was needed. Sandy went back to her room without saying a word. I covered Jess up and left the light on in the bathroom so she could find her way there. I lay back in bed, and although still pretty mad, reached over and patted her back. She mumbled something and passed out again.

About dawn, I heard retching in the bathroom and went in there to help. She was kneeling in front of the toilet emptying her stomach contents mostly into the toilet but had gotten some on her as well. I had made a good call on the old tee shirt. Her hair had gotten loose, and some of it was hanging down, getting vomit on it. I pulled what hair I could into the ponytail scrunchy thing and got it all out of the way, while I held her shoulders. She was done now, and groaning. I wiped her face, hair, and arms, then got another tee shirt and put it on her, dressing her like a sleepy child. I walked her back to the bed and put her back in position. I hated to see her this way, and my heart was breaking for her. I watched her for a long time as she went back to sleep.

In the morning, I was sitting at the kitchen table having coffee and staring at the walls. The airline called and was going to assign me to a trip. I told them I was caring for a sick family member and could not come to work. They marked me down for sick call and gave me instructions on what to do to get back on duty. I had never called in sick before.

Sandy came down dressed for work, carrying her suitcase. We just looked at each other. She left without saying a word. Eventually, Jess came downstairs, still wearing the last tee shirt I had put on her. She reeked of vomit and stale wine. She looked like shit. I could understand why. I offered her water, which she drank gratefully. She looked at me with glassy eyes. I looked back at her, not saying a word. Finally, she said, "I feel like shit. I'm so sorry about last night. What the fuck is wrong with me?"

Coldly, I said, "I have no idea what is wrong with you, Jess. You said some very hurtful things to me and your best friend. What caused all that? You've had bad days before."

She started crying softly. "I don't know, Dirk! All of a sudden, these past few days I felt like I was trapped in a never-ending spiral of depression. A guy hit on me during the trip, and I told him I was in a relationship, but not married. Then it hit me, that I'm never going to be married, so why be in an exclusive relationship? But it's because I love you! Oh, I'm so confused. I don't know what to do!" She put her head in her hands, sobbing.

I was coldly furious. "I'll help you out with what to do, Jess. First, find another place to live. Today. Then apologize to your best friend. Today. Then get some counseling. Find a place, today. Maybe I'll see you again sometime after you get your shit together. Right now, all I want is for you to get the fuck out of my sight. I'm sorry to be so rough on you, but I love you and you've hurt me as badly as I have ever been hurt. I hope you get some help. Now get your ass upstairs and get cleaned up and get out of here. You can come back for the rest of your shit some other time, or if I don't calm down, you'll find it on the lawn."

She nodded while sniffling and crying and went back upstairs. I heard the shower running, the same one where we had spent so many soapy fun times together. I heard her walking around, then she came down, got her uniform jacket out of the closet, picked up her suitcase where she had left it at the door last night, and walked out of my life, quietly shutting the door.

I put my head in my hands and wept. After a while, I dragged myself upstairs to lie down. I was exhausted emotionally and had not had much sleep. She had made the bed. I don't know why, but that made me cry again. I fell asleep and did not dream. When I awoke in mid-afternoon, I could feel the emptiness of the condo. It matched the emptiness in my heart. I had let another woman get under my skin after all these years, and she had broken my heart.

Back in action

I cleared sick call the next day and got assigned a Frankfurt, Germany trip for today on the same phone call. I dressed and headed for work, trying to concentrate. It was good to be back in the seat, and the comforting, solid feel of the big airplane helped my mood immensely. A night crossing of the North Atlantic Ocean has plenty of time for contemplation. This trip had a long layover, and the Captain and I had dinner and drinks together that night after a nap. We had flown together before, and he noted a change in my demeanor. He kindly asked if anything was wrong. It was all I could do to keep from crying. I just said, "Girl trouble," and left it at that.

Back home, I walked into a dark, empty condo. I went upstairs right away. All trace of Jess was gone. Sandy was gone, too. She had left her bed neatly made, clean sheets and all. A check for the balance of rent owed was on the table, and there was a note from Sandy saying she had mailed the keys to me. That was all. I was alone.

Months passed, with the only interesting thing besides flying was that I bought a houseboat on Lake Lanier, northeast of Atlanta, sight unseen. A 767 Captain I was flying with was going through a divorce and put a ridiculously low value on his boat as one of his possessions before the marriage. The judge called bullshit on that and demanded that he sell it for that value or face a fine for contempt of court, falsifying claims, etc. We were flying back from Europe when he told me about it. He showed me some pictures, and I bought it sight unseen during the flight for about a third of its value. I wrote him a post-dated check, called the military credit union as soon as I landed, and got an appraiser out the next day. The appraisal came in at what he claimed it was worth, and the credit union approved the loan the next day. I was a boat owner and had no idea why. Maybe having a boat would cheer me up.

I had friends out on the boat the next week, and we had a great time. During happy hour one day, they said I needed to give the boat a new name. I gave it some thought and named it the Busted Flush, after one of my fictional pulp fiction novel heroes by author John D. MacDonald. It fit.

I had not been interested in dating for a while. One day, I ran across a nice lady, and we clicked. I had a nice time with her and felt like I was getting back to normal.

A year passed, and I had successfully dated several times and then had several very nice experiences right in a row. After Tina, Kim, and Erika, the year was going well, but Jess was still a cloud hanging over me.

One day, I called Erika, who was by now a 71-year-old psychologist up in Boston. We had a lot of fun the previous year in Atlanta. She was a smart lady and had helped me out before. After catching up, she could tell something was wrong. I told her about Jess and how it had ended. Erika listened carefully and had some good comments.

"Dirk, you need closure. Contact Jess and have lunch together or something benign in a neutral setting and work it out. Since you were in love, that needs to be put to bed so to speak. You either have feelings for her still, or you don't. It's a binary choice."

I sighed into the phone. "I dunno, Doc. What if she wants to get back together? I'm not sure I could tell her no."

"You have no obligation to do that, Dirk. Tell yourself ahead of time that you just want to hear her side of the story. But, be open. Listen with your head, not your heart. Maybe there were extenuating circumstances that led to her meltdown. All humans have stress points. It sounds like she reached hers, and your reaction to break up immediately caused you to not hear the entire story."

"I keep thinking about that, Doc. I only heard a short version of why she was confused about our relationship. Maybe I should have waited and heard her out, or waited until she saw one of you head shrinkers."

She paused. "I think you may have found the solution, Dirk. Get some closure and be open."

I smiled at the phone. "You always make me feel better, Doc."

She laughed. "I'm glad to help. When are you coming to Boston to screw my brains out?"

It was my turn to laugh. "Soon, Doc. You know the planes fly both ways, right?"

"Yes, I know. My body shudders in girlish anticipation of the next time you put your hands on me."

I was still laughing. "Stop it, Doc. You're giving me a woody."

"That was the intention. Talk to the girl. But come screw me first in case you get involved again."

We set a tentative date to get reconnected, and I rang off. Erika always made me feel better. Maybe that was why she was a legend in her field. I would have to see her soon, for several reasons.

I went to Boston on my days off and reconnected with Erika, who was a delight in the sack and a great person to talk to. We had another great sexual experience and spent hours talking about life in general, and mine in particular. Erika was a perfect lady to date. All she wanted to do was experience sex and have fun, with no attachments.

The summer was winding down, and after Labor Day at the lake, I was ready to start thinking about a girl to keep me warm in the fall and winter. I had my eyes and ears open. I got a few vibes from girls I would be following up with. On September 10, 2001, I flew to Amsterdam, arriving on the morning of the 11th. We went to bed for a nap, to meet for dinner later. While we slept, America was attacked.

Furlough

As we turned on our TVs after our nap, we watched in horror at the constant replay of our brothers at American and United Airlines getting hijacked and then their planes used as weapons. Stunned, we called each other and met in the lounge. Our crew, along with crews from several other airlines hugged each other and commiserated. It was all anyone could talk about. Our Captain got through to dispatch. All flights into the US were grounded, and all air traffic was shut down. Several of our flights had to land in Canada, and their hundreds of passengers were taken in by local Canadians. We can never thank them enough. We talked for hours, with some of the flight attendants very upset. In the early evening, I felt I had to break the cycle of misery.

I called out to the room that I was opening up my room to be a safe haven away from the bad news of the day. I invited everyone to come up, we would get some drinks and snacks, order happy movies on pay-per-view and just hang out together and get away from the bad news. I announced that everyone should get dressed for bed and join me. Before I knew it, I had about 10 people in my room. Most had tee shirts and shorts on as I did, with some in regular pajamas or nightgowns. I let the ladies pick something light for a movie to watch and sent someone else to the bar for drinks. Soon, I was lying in bed with a woman curled up on each side of me, just cuddling and seeking human comfort. There were about three more flight attendants laying all over the bed, some on the floor, and some in the few chairs. We forgot about the stress of the day, and all calmed down. After a few movies, I fell asleep with one lady under each arm, their arms crossing my chest as we all went to sleep. It was very comforting and helped everyone.

The next day, the Captain got the plan from dispatch, and the day after that we headed back to Atlanta, with stringent security precautions in place. After landing, the flight attendants that I had over for 'movie night' as we called it hugged me and said thanks for helping them through a rough spot. Hell, they helped me, too.

There were things to be done. I had a bad feeling that the economy would tank, so even before movie night on the 11th, I got on to the website for my retirement funds and moved every penny into cash. From Amsterdam, I called a guy at my marina that was interested in buying my boat. I told him I was ready to sell, and he made me an okay but low offer, but it was in cash, so that made it worthwhile. I sold the boat and paid off my loan at the credit union with some extra money to put into savings.

Then I took my nice truck that I was making payments on to a used car dealer and walked away in an airport car that had seen better days. I was now debt free and ready for a shitty economy.

The airline decided the terrible losses associated with the attack were a good reason to reduce the employee force and started laying off employees as fast as they could. Being relatively junior, I was on the street after the third round of layoffs.

I had applied to the DeKalb County school system to be a substitute teacher, the only thing my four-year degree was good for. Then I went back to the flight school I had taught at and called all of my old students to see if they wanted to fly for old time's sake, and maybe get a higher rating or get some specialized training. Now I had some income, not much but better than nothing.

I went to a local thrift store and got a cheap bunk bed set and found two young instructors at the flight school to take in as tenants. I had an income stream and was in a good spot to survive the furlough. My retirement funds were safe, I had some cash, and I was in a good position. All I had to do was wait out the furlough.

The financial side was safe enough, but my personal life wasn't so great. My regular houseboat buddy Kim went back into the Air Force, got shipped out to Korea, and would never come back to Atlanta or the airline. Tina came to see me from Omaha, but it turned out to be a last fling for her as she was getting involved with a guy back home. Erika came down with a debilitating disease and had gone from a vibrant, healthy 72-year-old to an invalid in a short period. She didn't want me to see her like that, but we talked often.

For dating, there were lots of easy pickings among the young, single teachers I worked with. They were great for sex, but there was not a lot I had in common with them to talk about. Most single ladies my age had kids at home and were husband shopping. I spent a lot of time in my condo alone, just reading and listening to music.

Then Jess called me.

Attempted Closure

"Dirk? This is Jess."

My heart skipped a beat. Keep it cool, Dirk, seek closure like Doctor Erika had said. "Hey, Jess."

She hesitated. "I'd like to meet you for lunch sometime to talk."

"It's been almost two years, Jess. What do you need to talk about?"

She hesitated again. "I need to clear the air with you about our breakup."

This was just what Erika said needed to be done. "Well, okay. I'm working Monday through Friday as a substitute teacher and spend my weekends at the flight school. When did you have in mind?"

She laughed. "I'm working in a department store at Gwinnett Place Mall. I have Sundays and Mondays off."

We decided on Sunday at a chain restaurant at the mall. As we rang off, I had mixed feelings about what to expect. What would happen next?

I met her at the appointed time and place. She had cut her hair to a shorter style, and it was no longer the natural brown, being dyed a honey blond. She looked good, had not gained a pound, and may have lost a few. Her pretty blue eyes were as I remembered them from all the times I had been inches away from her face. Her mouth was fixed in a small smile. She looked calm. I thought a kiss was inappropriate given the way we had parted company, so I just stood there with my hands at my sides.

"Hello, Jess."

"Hello, Dirk. Thanks for meeting with me."

"I'm still not sure why I'm here."

"You're here because I asked you to listen to the reasons I have that caused our breakup."

I looked straight at her. "I imagine you are doing this on advice from a mental health professional to get closure."

She looked surprised. "Yes, that's right. I need to tell you these things to help both of us."

"Okay, Jess. Let's get an out of the way table and you can tell me your reasons."

We took a quiet table, and both ordered a diet soda. She tried to begin with small talk.

Smiling, she said, "How do you like substitute teaching?"

"I'm a pilot, I fucking hate it, what do you think? We're not here for chit-chat, Jess. Tell me what you have on your mind, and we'll get on with our lives."

The smile ran away from her face. She had some rehearsed lines, and I was screwing things up. She started trying to get back to her script, which I imagine her counselor had helped her with. She began by saying she had been confused about our relationship and then did not know if she wanted to get married or continue just living together, and when she saw Sandy and I together like a couple, she got drunk and said things she shouldn't have. She paused, waiting for my reaction.

My temper was rising. I sat there for a minute then laid into her. "Jess, that is such bullshit. You had been tempted to cheat on me and then had trust issues with yourself about whether or not you could continue to be faithful. Then you thought if you had trust issues, surely, I must have the same problem. Then in some fucked up way, you imagined me cheating on you, even with your best friend. You got sloppy drunk after a shitty trip, and it all came out. You didn't just say things you shouldn't have, you said incredibly hurtful things to me and your friend that can never be unsaid. I did not hear one word of apology or regret in your little speech. This isn't closure, it's a fucking half-truth and you are not taking ownership of your actions. I'll bet you did not tell your counselor about having thoughts of cheating, did you?"

Tears were streaming down her cheeks. She shook her head no.

I kept going. "Damn it, Jess! You need to come clean with that counselor. That's the only way you will get any relief. You know the truth and still came here with some shitty story that is only a band-aid for your conscience. I'm sitting here looking at a beautiful woman that I loved and really needed for support with the furloughs and all the shit going on. You should have talked to me about your concern about wanting to cheat. All couples look outside their relationship or marriage and feel tempted sometimes. We would have worked it out. We could have gotten couples therapy. We should have been together all this time. It's like all the time we had together was wasted."

Jess was sobbing openly by now. The waitress appeared, looking concerned. I told her, "We're having closure," and she ran away.

Between sobs, Jess was trying to talk. "Oh, Dirk! I'm so sorry! I thought we would talk and then maybe get back together!"

I shook my head. "No way, Jess. You broke my heart once and I'm not inclined to give you another shot. You need to get your shit together and admit to yourself that you have trust issues with yourself. I'm not sure you can ever have a committed relationship. Give me a call after that, and we'll talk again."

I threw some money on the table to cover the soft drinks we hadn't touched. "Come on, Jess. I'll walk you to your car. You're a mess."

We walked out to her car, and I watched her get in and drive away after she got herself together. Shaking my head, I went back to my beat-up old car, still seething with anger at the woman I still loved. This had not been a very satisfying visit. No closure was detected that I could discern.

I had some trouble with depression after that. The VA had counselors who were good dudes to talk with, and I joined a discussion group. That helped a lot. I had banged my way through just about every willing female in the DeKalb County school system, including one principal. I'll have to write a story about that someday. I was getting worse about staying at home, and not doing anything except work to pay the bills. Then one day my friend and fellow furloughed pilot Jason called.

Back in the saddle

"Dirk! I fell into a management job with a start-up charter company flying 757s and 767s! They are hiring pilots to fill Captain seats with 767 type-rated guys. I thought of you, do you want in?"

"This is the first I have heard of this company, Jason. What's it like?"

Jason laughed. "It's long hours and shitty pay. We fly all over the world, filling in for other small airlines when a plane goes into scheduled maintenance, or they need additional seasonal service. I'm off to Norway next week with one plane, and the other is doing service in the Caribbean. We're adding another plane and need crews badly."

I was intrigued. "That sounds a lot better than substitute teaching, Jason. Whom do I call for an interview?"

He laughed again. "You just had your interview, I'm the freaking Chief Pilot! I'll send you some stuff. Plan on a class date for ground school in about 10 days."

We rang off, and for the first time in a long time, I whistled as I went about my condo. Back in an airliner cockpit at last. I felt like my old self again.

Flying as a Captain for the charter company was very different from my airline. They operated on a shoestring budget, and some of the places we went had never seen an American registered airplane before. At one airport in Africa, I had to go count the fire trucks and see if they had firefighting foam in them before the governing authority would let us operate. I flew to Africa, South America, the Caribbean, Northern Europe, and Asia. We had a long contract in Turkey, where I found out some of the local women were sizzling hot. That may be another book, just describing that experience.

Our flight attendants came in all shapes, sizes, ages, colors, and temperaments. We had a flight attendant base in New York and another in Oakland. While I had several offers, I stayed the hell away from sleeping with any of our flight attendants. I did not need any more flight attendant drama in my life. I was happy and busy, and it turned out the charter world was a lot of fun. We did golf charters to Mexico and flew NBA sports teams with celebrity players that were entertaining.

Back in Atlanta, my airline had stopped furloughing and started recalling pilots and flight attendants. It would be a long time before they got to my seniority number, so I kept busy and somewhat sane flying around the world until they got to me. After one charter trip about six months after recalls had started, I got home and found a form in my mailbox from the post office to come to sign for a certified letter. I raced to the post office and opened it in my car. It was from the airline, offering a recall on a certain date. I called the flight office and accepted verbally and had to send them a reply letter for formal acceptance. The class date for ground school to get requalified would be the following month. My furlough lasted around two years.

I had recall rights to the 767, but that did not include any base rights. I went back to New York, and back to crash pad life. I came home infrequently, there just was no reason to make the commute back to an empty condo. The pilot union had made a good deal on our pay rates, and I was enjoying a good increase in salary, which I was banking and investing most of.

When airlines respond to a changing economy, their manning goes through some tremendous swings. We had so many senior guys take early retirement, and guys senior to me moving to new airplanes or finding other jobs, that Captain bids were suddenly going very junior. I bid for and got a Captain slot on the old MD-80 in New York. I hoped to be back in Atlanta soon.

I loved the job and the responsibility and felt the time I had been flying as a Captain at the charter job helped me to prepare. After a year or so of crash pad life, I got an assignment back to Atlanta and what home I had. When the latest round of my young instructor tenants went on to other jobs, I did not replace them. I sold the bunk beds for what I had paid for them years before and restored the second bedroom to its previous state. I also had the kitchen and dining area floors redone and changed the paint scheme of the whole place to a more modern look. I had the countertops replaced with nice granite and replaced the fixtures and appliances. The carpeting was replaced with newer, more contemporary colors. My furniture was still in good shape, except for the wine stain on the couch. I decided to recover the couch to get rid of that memory. I was pleased with the result. I was in my mid-50s by then and my home had a new look, I had a great job, and I was reasonably happy.

One day, I was getting ready to fly up to Albany, NY after an Orlando round trip. I would be changing planes and concourses as usual in Atlanta, getting a new flight attendant crew, and then hustling up to Albany for the overnight layover. The first officer and I arrived at the gate, where they were ready to load. I held the gate agent off for a minute while I went down to brief the flight attendants. I gathered them up, pulled out my briefing guide, and waited as the lead flight attendant introduced herself and her crew.

"Captain, I'm Sue. This is Dana, and this is Jess, who will be our number three, in the back."

I looked up and found myself staring into Jess' blue eyes.

Together again

I found my voice after a moment. "Hello, Sue and Dana. Nice to meet you. I know Jess already. How are you doing?"

Sue and Dana nodded and said hi. Jess smiled and said calmly, "Hello, Captain. It's nice to see you again."

I turned to Sue. "Go ahead and start boarding when you are ready. Jess, can I speak to you on the jet bridge for a moment?"

She joined me outside the airplane. We were as alone as we could be. I said, "Jess, are you all right flying with me? Will there be any problems based on our past?"

She shook her head. "No, Dirk. I've got it all together. I won't be any trouble."

I looked at her. She looked great, as always. "Thanks."

She continued, "Maybe we can find some time to talk in Albany. I'd like to tell you some things."

"I'd like that, Jess. We'll make time for that."

With that, we got busy and took a load of people to Albany. During the flight, Jess came to the flight deck to bring us some coffee and handed me a folded slip of paper while smiling at me. The first officer had noticed and asked with a smile on his face if I was passing love notes back and forth with the flight attendants.

"No, it says the copilot is cute, can she have your phone number?"

He laughed, "Darn it, I'm married."

I opened the note. It had a phone number and her name, and said, "Please text me when we get to the hotel, so we can meet to talk." I folded it and put it in my book bag for safekeeping. I thought about what we would talk about. Did she have more on why we had broken up? I sighed. I'd find out soon enough. The two-hour flight seemed like it was taking forever.

We got everyone to the airport on time and put the plane to bed. We would be taking it back to Atlanta first thing in the morning, on a minimum rest overnight schedule, quite common for domestic flights. There would be no happy hour tonight. Arriving at the airport hotel, I passed out the room keys and headed up to mine. Once there, I texted Jess, "Where and when to talk?"

She replied at once. "Lobby, 30 minutes?" I sent back a thumbs up. I was getting quite good at these new phones. I changed into my layover attire, thinking that I wished I had brought a nicer shirt. In the lobby a few minutes early, I saw Jess there, waiting by herself. She said, "Let's head out the door and find a place before someone else comes down and wants to join us."

"Good idea."

We were at the Marriott by the airport, and I knew there were steakhouse chains a few blocks to the west. "Outback or Longhorns? They are across the street from each other."

Jess laughed. "What's on our side of the street."

"Outback."

"Outback it is, then."

We walked in silence, each not sure of what to say. We asked the server for a quiet table, and we sat across from one another in a booth. We each ordered a diet soda and contemplated each other for a moment. Her hair was shorter than the last time I had seen her, years before, and was a darker blond than I recalled. Her face had a few more lines but was still very pretty. The blue eyes were framed by conservative eyeliner and eye shadow. She wore nice red lipstick and a familiar gold necklace. Her arms were still firm, and her swimmer's shoulders were still straight and strong. Her hands had some veins showing, and she wore no rings on her fingers with manicured and painted nails. She had worn slacks and a blouse, so I had no idea what her legs looked like now, but I imagined they were still firm, with some tan. Let's see, if I am 55, she was ... 43?

She smiled at me and broke the ice. "You're getting grey hair. It looks good on you, I like it."

"It drives the older ladies crazy with desire. You look good, Jess. How have you been?"

She nodded. "Good, Dirk. Really good. I've made some changes in my life." She paused for a minute, and gathered her thoughts, then continued. "I'd like to start by apologizing for the terrible way I acted when we broke up. That was uncalled for, and I've embraced the reason I was such a bitch to you and Sandy that awful night."

I nodded, letting her get it all out.

She continued, "You were almost exactly right when we had that discussion at Gwinnett Mall. I was doubting my ability to be faithful and somehow in my head convinced myself you were screwing around on me. I know now you weren't, and I feel ashamed for saying those things. I hope you can forgive me."

I nodded again, not trusting myself to speak without choking up.

"Last year, a nice lady psychologist from Boston called me. She said she was a friend of yours. We had some great discussions and she helped me get through this. I owe her a lot."

I swallowed hard. How on earth did Erika find Jess? I managed to say, "Erika is a great lady."

Jess nodded and went quiet. I waited. After a minute, she continued.

"I'd been trying to work up the nerve to call you and tell you these things. I was so afraid you would still be angry with me for treating you so badly. I should have talked to you long before this."

It was my turn. "I'm not going to lie. I was terribly angry with you, Jess. I'm very glad you have it all straight in your head now and decided to tell me what was on your mind. I forgive you." I waited a minute, gathering the courage to say what I had been waiting so long to tell her. "I love you, Jessica."

She smiled shyly. "It still gives me shivers when you say my whole name." She locked eyes with me. "I love you, too, Dirk."

Just at that tender moment, the server came by to tell all about the wonderful specials. We started to order, when Jess chimed in, "You should get the small steak, Dirk, And skip the potato and get vegetables instead."

I looked up at her and smiled. "Still bossy."

She blushed. "I'm sorry. Old habits die hard."

I looked at the server and ordered as Jess suggested.

Alone again, I had to ask. "What's your status? No wedding or engagement ring, I see. Are you seeing anyone? Sorry to be intrusive."

She smiled. "It's okay to ask. I've had some dates, but nothing serious. That was mostly not wanting to be alone."

We sat in silence for a minute, both afraid to ask the other. Finally, I summoned the courage. "Would you like to start dating again? Me, that is. Damn, that sounds awkward."

She reached her hand across the table. I touched her for the first time in years. We held hands and enjoyed the moment. "That's a yes, isn't it?" she nodded, and her eyes teared up.

"We'll have to take it slowly, Jess. I don't want to screw this up."

She nodded again, and smiling through her tears said, "Does this mean I shouldn't show up unannounced at your hotel room and throw myself at you, like in Buffalo when we first met?"

"While that would be fun, that's the opposite of taking it slowly."

She managed to laugh, blew her nose, and was fine after that. We finished dinner slowly, shared a dessert, and strolled back to the hotel holding hands. It felt like we had come home.

Next steps

We parted after a brief kiss in the elevator, promising to coordinate a date in Atlanta. The next morning, the entire crew met at the curb for the van ride to the hotel. Everyone chatted as they compared notes on where they went for dinner. We woke the plane up, loaded it with people, and jetted off for the two-hour flight back to the base. The pilots were heading to Dallas for an overnight, while the flight attendants were going to do a New York round trip and then be done. I would not be back in Atlanta until the following day.

During the flight, Jess came to the flight deck again under the guise of bringing coffee, but she handed me a larger piece of paper, winked at the first officer, and left. The first officer looked at me. "More love notes?"

I looked at the sheet of paper. She had written down all of her days off and put a cute little heart on the bottom. "This time, it's a written request for all my assets to see if I am worthy of dating." He laughed delightedly.

"You could do worse. She's a peach."

I smiled, "Yes, she is." I smiled all the way to Atlanta.

After landing and parking, we were packing up to go to our next gate, when the intercom chimed. The first officer answered, then handed me the handset. "It's Jess in the back for you."

I took the handset and said, "Dirk here."

She said, "I'm stuck in the back and won't be able to say goodbye in person and you guys have to leave. You don't have to say anything back because I know you're not alone. I love you, Dirk. Call me."

The first officer was looking at me oddly. I managed to answer, "Thanks. I'll look forward to that."

He was looking at me quizzically. I said, "She thanked us for a nice flight and hopes to fly with us again."

He shook his head. "She is really nice. That's the first time any flight attendant has said that. That makes me feel good."

I smiled, "Me, too."

I finished the trip, having coordinated a date night with Jess when I got to Dallas. We would meet in a few days for dinner at a restaurant in town. I suggested Joey D's where we had eaten before since it was kind of a celebration, and she happily agreed. We talked a few times in the days between. She was cheerful and buoyant, seemingly eager to be together again.

It felt funny, meeting Jess at the restaurant for a dinner date. We had lived together for a while, been intimate many times, and shared laughter and tears. Now we were starting over. She showed up exactly on time, looking great in a nice light blue dress and jacket, making her eyes pop. She wore sparkly earrings to match her necklace, and dark red lipstick accentuated her makeup.

I kissed her lightly to not smear her lipstick. "You look beautiful, Jess."

She dimpled and blushed a little. "Thanks, I wanted to look nice for you on our first date in a long time."

We ordered wine and looked at each other. We both started to speak at once and then we laughed. She said, "Go ahead."

I said, "It feels a little funny being on a date when we used to live together."

Nodding, she said, "I feel it, too. Like a new beginning?"

"Yes, that's it. A fresh start."

The wine came. I raised my glass. "To a fresh start."

She smiled and clinked glasses. "Hear, hear!"

We sipped the wine in silence for a while. Then she said, "Tell me what you have been doing since I saw you last. Is that too broad a subject?"

I told her about a lot of things, trying to stay on the light side. We had plenty of time to go in-depth later. She was fascinated by my stories of the charter airline and the different places I had been, the people I carried, and the sports figures.

Our dinner had come and gone while I was talking. "Now tell me about you."

She had worked at a large chain department store for a long time during the furlough and had visited her parents, and her nieces and nephews. She did not have a lot to say. "I just worked and kept my expenses down until I got recalled. I got some help from a therapist, which helped some, and then Erika helped me even more. I slowly began to get my shit together, then went back to work when my head was straight. I started flying domestically about a year ago. That's about it. Pretty boring stuff compared to you."

I thought for a minute, then added some detail. "In full disclosure, I saw a therapist at the VA for help with depression after 9/11, the furlough, and what we were going through. They helped me a lot."

She just nodded understandingly. "Thanks, Dirk. You didn't have to share that."

I shook my head, "No, I need to share everything with you."

She reached for my hand and said softly, "Are you going to be able to let me back in your heart, Dirk?"

I held back tears. "You've never left my heart, amore mio."

She blinked back tears as well. "I'll never hurt you again, mio caro. I promise."

I smiled. "I'm going to hold you to that."

After a minute, to lighten the mood, I said, "Now that I am a Captain, we don't have to go to Denny's for dessert."

She laughed. "No, I want to! That's our routine. Fine dining, then budget dessert!"

We drove to Denny's, shared a dessert, and lingered over coffee. She looked up and smiled.

I was curious. "What's the smile for?"

"A couple of things. First, I'm happy, you big dork. Secondly, I'm suddenly feeling shy about telling you something."

"Nobody's called me a big dork in a while, thanks for that. What are you shy about?"

She leaned close and whispered, "I have an overnight bag in my car."

Ever the comedian, I whispered back, "Are you going on a trip?"

She punched me in the shoulder while laughing. "Yeah, I thought I'd go to a condo in Norcross and see if someone would offer me a nightcap."

"I can do that." Then I felt serious. "Is it too soon? Are we ready for that emotional roller coaster that comes with that?"

She held my hand and locked eyes. "I'm willing to try, my love," she said quietly.

I waved at the server. "Check, please!"

We drove separately to the condo. As we walked up to the entrance, I asked her, "Is this going to be hard for you? We've had some great times here, but the last time you were here was the breakup."

She looked brave. "I think I'll be okay. We'll see. We have to do it sometime."

I opened the door and let us in. She immediately noticed the updates. "Oh, wow! I love it! Dirk! It's a complete makeover!"

She walked through on her own, gawking. "Incredible! You've increased the resale value of this place by half again!"

Then she came to me and gave me a big hug and kiss. "It's like a new beginning for our new beginning."

It felt right to have my arms around her. We stayed like that for a minute, then I said, "Welcome home, Jessica."

She looked at me, took my face in both her hands, and couldn't speak. She nodded and tried to smile, but a wracking sob escaped her, and she started crying. I held her and stroked her back and hair, trying to comfort her. "What's wrong, honey? Bad memories?"

After a minute, she was able to speak. "Good memories. So many good ones." She sniffled. "I've missed you so much!"

I started crying, too. After a few minutes of snorting and sniffling, we both wiped our eyes and smiled at each other. I said, "That's not how we used to start a romantic evening."

She was laughing and sniffling at the same time. "Always the comedian, Caldwell. May I have some wine, please?"

"Coming right up."

As we sat on the couch and calmed down, she suddenly got serious. "Dirk, every time I have more than a couple of drinks, I don't want you to worry about if I am going to have another homewrecking meltdown or not. I'm good now, and I want you to be confident that I am. You'll have to see for yourself, but I wanted to say that."

"Thanks. I didn't even think about that."

She nodded. "I want all our cards on the table, Dirk. I think I'm going to be fine now. The place is so different, it feels new to me."

"Good."

We chatted about this and that, like old times. When we finished our wine, she collected the glasses and rinsed them in the sink. She came back with a big smile. "Want me to walk up the stairs in front of you?"

"Yes, please!"

She did, and her ass looked as good as ever. When we got to the top, she took her bag from me and said, "I'm going to use ... Sandy's bathroom for a minute."

"It's just the guest bath now."

She nodded, still seeing ghosts.

I went into the master bedroom, turned a small light on, and pulled back the bedspread, revealing new and very high thread count sheets. I visited the bathroom, and she reappeared as I came out. She was wearing a gossamer thin light purple nightie set, a jacket over a thin, see-through bra, and string see-through panties. I felt my cock waking up.

"Wow, Jess! You look fantastic!"

She smiled widely. "This is the premiere event for this outfit. I bought it this week, hoping you might like it."

"I like it a lot, but you may not have it on for long."

She moved into the room and did a model's pirouette. "That's the idea, amore mio."

I took her in my arms and held her while running my hands all over her, getting reacquainted with her textures, sights, and scents. Her ass was still firm, and when I ran my hands over her breasts, she had a sharp intake of breath.

"Captain, you have too many clothes on for this operation. I'm going to have to help you."

"I must say that's the first time I've heard that."

"That, my good man, is the diplomatic and most correct answer."

Then she pulled back for a second and looked serious. "Dirk, I know you've had other women since me. You had to. I'm not judging that at all. I'm here now, that's all you need to think about. Get all those women out of your head, and be with me, body and soul."

"Very well and poetically put. I think you were undressing me?"

"Ah! Thanks for the reminder."

She slowly and tantalizingly undressed me. I ran my hands over her as she did so, savoring her body and kissing her. It felt great. She had me naked soon and folded my clothes neatly and placed them on the dresser. I had forgotten that quirk.

We lay together, and I caressed her boobs and admired them.

"Do you think they have started to sag?"

There is no good answer to that question. "They're beautiful, like you."

She laughed. "Smooth talker!"

I kissed her up and down her torso, and ran my fingertips over the thin panties, feeling her labia as I did so. She closed her eyes, and her lips parted a little. I slid my hand under the panties and put my finger between the lips, then moved it up and down. Most pussies feel the same, but hers was much nicer. I may have been prejudiced. She moaned a little. I loved that sound from her. I tickled the clit, and she squirmed in response. A bit later, I put my finger into her, curled it, and found the G spot right away. She drew in her breath sharply, then moaned.

"Damn, Dirk. You know right where that spot is ... Ohhhh!"

I was squeezing her nipples a little and she liked that, too. Then I untied the string bra and let her boobs loose. They got some attention as I continued to work up and down her slit. I untied the panties as she moaned some more. She opened her eyes and looked at me.

"I know we are both excited, but ..."

"Give you some head? I am on it."

She laid back with a smile. "You know me so well."

I knelt between her legs and spread her wide open. I put my head down to her pussy and appreciated the scent, the textures, and her beautiful labia. I spread the labia and inserted my tongue into the pink flesh of her wide-open cunt. She groaned and squirmed. I then went to the top of the slit and rolled my tongue like a straw and applied some suction to the erect clitoris. Her hips bucked, and a loud moan emanated. I went down straight to her hole, went far in, and curled my tongue to tickle the G spot. She groaned, and her hands flew to my head, pushing me deeper. I kept at that for a minute, to louder and louder groans and increased hip wiggling and squirming. She gasped, "Oh, Dirk! I've missed this!"

I slid up and moved my hips up to hers and put the head of my cock at the labia. She was right there guiding me in. I slowly thrust forward and back a few times, lubricating my cock in her wet pussy. Then with one thrust, I went all the way in. She gasped, and her eyes opened wide.

She locked eyes with me, then pulled me to her for a deep kiss while I was all the way in her. Then she said, "Now, you're home, Dirk."

I started thrusting gently in and out as her hips moved into mine. I had missed her motion and answering pushes. Nobody was better at it than she. I looked at her face and was surprised to see tears running down her cheeks. I reached up to wipe her eyes. "Hey, sweetheart. What's wrong?"

She smiled while crying. "I'm just so happy!"

I could handle that. We kept up a gentle rhythm, enjoying the intimacy and feelings, while our emotions ran the scale. After a few minutes, she moved her hands so that one was on my ass, pulling me in, and the other was on my hair, caressing me. The pressure built, and I groaned heavily as I shot my load into her, and while that was going on, she cried out in ecstasy and buried her face in my neck, and showered me with kisses. We had reunited and had an orgasm together after far too long.

Spent, I lay on her for a minute while she kissed me nonstop and murmured sweet love words. I rolled off her to see her smiling at me, which seemed at odds with the tracks of tears on her cheeks. I kissed each one of her eyelids, her nose, her chin, and then her lips. She smiled and smiled. We snuggled together like we had not been apart for a day. I caressed her boobs, ass, back, and hair. I looked into her eyes and said, "I love you, dear Jessica." Her eyes teared up again, so I kissed them dry. We were both home.

Going International

I was lucky in love it seemed, then the company assignment fairy smiled upon me and awarded me a slot I never thought I would attain. I was now designated a Boeing 767 Captain in the International Division based in Atlanta. I was walking on clouds. My training date was almost immediate, and I was soon back on the campus relearning my old friend, the 767. I breezed through the simulator phase and had a quick check ride. I was able to mentor a first officer who was new to the jet and felt like the old pro I had developed into. Jess would try and bid for the international side so we could go on trips together, but her seniority meant that some of the old birds would have to move on before she could do so. She was happy for me, and that was the main concern.

I had a few overwater trips with a check airman, who observed the skills I had developed on the fly at the charter company and had no questions, except why he had to fly with me during another ocean crossing when I was already proficient. I soon was on my own, with scheduling setting me up with a month of trips for consolidation of skills. After that, I would be on reserve, but at home. It was a sweet deal. Jess took some days off and flew with me to Frankfurt on one trip, and we had fun looking at the sights together. The month of scheduled trips was done, and then I was at home waiting for scheduling to call. Such is the life of being junior in your bid status.

Jess and I had settled into a domestic state of bliss. After much discussion, it was decided that we would not live together for a while, to give our feelings and emotions time to settle down. We still spent a lot of time together, either at the condo or her place. It worked out well. Nobody mentioned the marriage word, and we blissfully engaged in loving each other, making up for lost time.

Jess and I went out to Lake Lanier together and looked at my old houseboat, still tied up in the same place. I was wanting another boat, so we put the word out that I was looking. In the fall, a very nice 80-foot boat became available as the result of the owners passing away. I knew the family from my time on the lake, and they offered me the boat at a ridiculously low price. They said their parents Jack and Donna really liked me and would want me to have the boat. I took the deal, feeling a little guilty. J&D had been good friends, and they befriended whatever girl I had at the lake with grace and decorum, with Jack especially enjoying them if they had a skimpy bikini on. They were good folks, and I would miss them. I vowed to make a Manhattan cocktail in Papa Jack's honor as he would every Friday we were there. We moved into the boat and enjoyed fall on the lake.

I was getting called out a fair bit on international trips, and Jess was independent enough not to be upset about me being gone. A year passed, and then another year. and we were still crazy about each other. Maybe this thing was going to work.

The company was happy with the way I mentored new first officers and put me into training to become a check airman. I enjoyed the duty and the extra pay and developed a reputation as the go-to guy for pilots who were struggling. Before I knew it, I had been a 767 Captain for five years, and I turned 60 years old on a trip. The FAA had recently changed the mandatory retirement age to 65, which I planned on making if my health stayed good.

Jess finally got into the international division and bid for and got the lead flight attendant or purser position on many trips, mainly because the older ladies did not want the extra workload. We started flying together a couple of times a month, and after she had seen all the sights at the various destinations as I had, we settled into a routine of being layover buddies and spending a lot of time together at our favorite restaurants or coffee shops in various cities like Rome, Frankfurt, Amsterdam, London, Paris, Madrid, Moscow, Stockholm and the like. It was comforting to have my life partner with me at international destinations. I was slowing down a little, and having Jess with me to keep me focused and active was a bonus.

Time passed quickly, and before I knew it, I was in my last year of flying. Too soon, the end would approach, and I'd suit up for one final trip. That day came all too soon, and Jess and I loaded our suitcases, and I made one last trip to the airport wearing my Captain's uniform a week before my 65th birthday and mandatory retirement.

Last Trip

The leg over to Rome for my last trip had an unexpected and emotional component as we stumbled upon my dear friend and mentor Gabriella on the flight. While we had a nice visit inflight, Jess found out Gabby was dying and making her final trip home to her beloved Italy. The crew was emotional over that and my retirement.

On a lighter note, while my large crew was waiting to go through customs, I looked up and saw a familiar smiling face. The cabin crew of an international airline flight is huge, and when the pilots board, we usually don't see all of the crew as they are scattered around the plane doing their thing. I made eye contact with a familiar face.

"Nancy! What the hell?" It was Nancy, the flight attendant supervisor who trained Jess on our first airline flight over 20 years ago. She was my age and was now a manager in the flight department. "I had no idea ..."

She laughed as we hugged, and she kissed my cheek. "Jess and I wanted to surprise you. We worked this out at the start of the bid period when we figured out this would be your last flight. I stayed in the back of the plane and was hoping you didn't see my name on the crew roster." She waved her arm at the gaggle of now-smiling flight attendants. "At least 10 flight attendants that you have known over the years bid this flight to fly with you on your last trip, and I arranged things with scheduling to make it happen."

I looked at the smiling faces, all familiar. "Thanks to you all for joining me! It means more than you can ever know."

We herded through customs and went to the curb for the hotel van. The hotel manager was there, beaming. I was shocked and went to shake his hand. "Marco! What are you doing at the airport?"

He replied with a grin, "Ciao, Capitano! For your last stay with us, I have arranged the special vehicle!" He indicated a Mercedes limo, waiting with the doors open. "Signorina Jessica wanted this to be a special day!"

I looked at Jess, who was grinning from ear to ear. "Thanks very much! Okay, let's go! Pack as many flight attendants as we can in here with us!" About five of my friends piled in, and we sat cheek to cheek in the special car, with them all chattering happily about the excitement, forgetting about the sadness of Gabby earlier. That's the way it should be, I thought as we drove to the hotel in style.

We gathered together in the lobby of our layover hotel, and Jess made an announcement. "Everyone! We will have a happy hour for Dirk starting at 1700 local. It will last for one hour and one hour only so we can get to dinner and get our rest. Glasses down by 2200 if you are having wine with dinner, so we can be legal for our trip home. We have a noon pickup time tomorrow. See you all there!"

The hotel manager had been briefed on my retirement by Jess, and he had gone all out with a VIP suite for her and me, along with a meeting room for the happy hour. He escorted us to the suite, and for the first time ever, a bellman carried our suitcases. In the elevator, Jess turned to me and gave me a quick kiss, our long-standing tradition. Marco beamed with joy. He's Italian, they kiss a lot.

The huge suite had a fruit basket, chocolate-covered strawberries, and a bottle of wine on the dining table. I turned to Marco and embraced him. "Grazie, amico mio. This is very nice."

He smiled and embraced Jess and went to leave. "Prego! It is my pleasure, Capitano. I leave you to rest before the party."

Finally alone, I turned to Jess. "Thanks for going to all this trouble."

She put her arms around me and kissed me deeply. "You deserve it, you big dork. Let's change and take a nap."

"Will there be fooling around before or after this nap?"

She laughed. "Save your energy, old man. You may need it tonight."

"That sounds promising."

We curled up together in the huge bed and had a nice nap. I always liked a nap after an ocean crossing to rest up for a nice evening. Our flight didn't leave until after 1300 local time, so it would be a leisurely layover.

We had a fun happy hour, and Marco had staffed the party with several of our favorite bartenders and waiters. I got to visit with friends I had known all my time at the airline, keeping it light and reminiscing about fun experiences together. Later, we went to dinner at one of our favorite restaurants nearby and enjoyed the company of the pilots and several flight attendants. Atlanta Assistant Chief Pilot Jim, who was flying as my first officer, picked up the tab. He grinned, "On behalf of the Chief Pilot and management staff, even though you gave us plenty of grief over the years." I had to laugh. He was right, I was always giving them crap about something, especially after I became a Check Airman.

I said, "Jim, I'm sorry to bite your head off earlier today when you asked if Jess and I were an item. Of course, we are and have been for years. It just hit me wrong."

Jim smiled and said, "Not a problem, Dirk. I shouldn't have said anything, besides, anyone can see the way you two look at each other and know."

Over coffee, some stories began to come out. Darlene had one.

"Dirk, do you remember years ago when I was a brand new lead attendant on the MD-80? On one flight out of LaGuardia, the catering was all screwed up, something needed to be cleaned in the cabin, and we were going to be late. I was frazzled. The gate agent was giving me grief, yelling at me to hurry up over and over. I heard a clank as your seat belts hit the floor and you practically jumped out of your seat, then you came back, and told the gate agent 'Come with me!' then took her out on the jetbridge."

Jess and Jim chuckled. "What happened then?"

Darlene laughed. "Dirk stood there with his arms crossed and asked the gate agent if the plane could depart with him standing on the jet bridge. Of course, the agent said no. Then Dirk said this was where he was going to be standing until his flight attendants got ready, so the agent could just wait there, too, and quit harassing them."

We all laughed. Darlene had more. "The gate agent went scurrying off to get her supervisor, and then a man in a grey suit carrying a clipboard and walkie-talkie showed up a few minutes later, demanding to know what the problem was."

Jim said, "Oh, no!"

Darlene continued, "Oh, yes! Dirk got right up in this guy's face with his hands on his hips and said something like if you management assholes would leave us alone, we could be doing our jobs, and that we all knew the goal of getting out on time, so why don't you just leave us the fuck alone! The guy ran off, and we got done and left almost on time."

The table dissolved into laughter. Jim said, "That's classic Dirk behavior. Don't mess with my crew, take no prisoners."

Storytelling continued over coffee, then Jess announced we were heading off to bed. With hugs all around, we said goodnight. We got back to our suite at a reasonable time, then relaxed on our sofa for a while, after kicking our shoes off. I had my arm around the love of my life, after a fun evening and a great meal. It was heavenly. We chatted quietly for a while, then I started yawning. At my age, all this excitement was taking a toll on my old body. Jess read the signs and announced that we would sleep now, and if I played my cards right, I would get lucky in the morning.

"You always have been bossy."

"I'm not bossy, I'm a natural leader. I keep telling you that."

"Why don't you put on short shorts, a tank top with no bra, and come to bed? I'll wake up sufficiently to do you properly."

She laughed. "I wore that for you twenty years ago when I was shamelessly wanting carnal knowledge with you. My boobs and ass are too saggy for that now."

"You are still sexy enough to make grown men paw the ground."

She looked at me and smiled. "It seems that you are perking up. Do you want it now or in the morning?"

"How about both?"

She smiled. "We aren't as young as we think we are, Dirk."

"Okay, now in that case."

She kept smiling and went off to the bathroom, returning in a few minutes wearing the negligee she wore on the night of our reunion.

"Wow! I remember that outfit. You look fantastic!"

She did the sexy model turn in front of me. "Why don't you come here and see what it feels like?"

I did, and my nearly 65-year-old weenie liked the way things looked, too. We embraced as I ran my hands all over her, enjoying the feel of her warm flesh under the flimsy garment. I cupped her breasts, feeling the erect nipples under the thin material. I slipped my hands under her panties and fondled her ass, still very cute. Then, while kissing her deeply, I pulled her tightly to me, and then led her to the bed.

Laying together, we caressed each other as long-time lovers do, gently finding the spots that each other liked. Our passion rose, and before long, I untied the panties and pulled them free. My hand went to her pussy, already damp with excitement, my finger stroking her labia gently, causing her to moan. I inserted the finger into her and went straight to her favorite spot, causing her hips to move and making her groan with pleasure. After tickling her G spot for a while, I moved to kneel between her legs.

With her watching me with a smile on her face, I gently spread her legs wide, running my hands slowly down the inside of her thighs. I moved closer and, as always, admired the view. Her breasts were still shapely at age 53, sagging a little but that was expected. Her stomach was almost flat, with just a little more flesh than 20 years ago. The chin had a little fleshiness, but it was barely noticeable. The blue eyes were wide open and sparkling with excitement. She was a remarkably beautiful woman, and I was extremely grateful that she was mine. I had better get to work.

Slowly, I put my face down to her warm, damp pussy after kissing her thighs all over. I savored the scent and the textures as I buried my face into the delightful patch of pubic hair, then slowly licked my way into her labia. My tongue parted the lips and went into the pink flesh, causing her to gasp. I went up to the clit, sucking it gently. Her hips were moving into my face now. I went straight to the hole, my tongue going deep and then curling to the G spot. She exclaimed, and pulled at my head with both hands, making my face and tongue go deeper into her. I peeked up at her face. The eyes were closed now, and her lips were parted, with constant moans coming out of her mouth.

I pulled back and kissed her all over her thighs, knees, ankles, and feet. I then took one of her big toes into my mouth and sucked it. She was going crazy. She gasped, "Stop that, or I'll come before you fuck me!"

I crawled back up to lay with her, then she pushed me on my back, bent over at the waist, and put my cock in her mouth, starting an enthusiastic blow job. I was rock hard by then, and my groans as she rolled her tongue around my shaft filled the room. After a few minutes of that very enjoyable activity, she raised up, then rolled onto her back and spread her legs. "Come on! Get on me!"

I knelt between her legs, and she guided my wet and throbbing manhood into her. As I eased all the way in, she gasped, "Oh Dirk! It's harder than it has been in a long time! Fuck me, baby! Fuck me hard!"

With that guidance, I started pumping away into her, faster and faster. She wanted it harder. "Harder! Fuck me harder, honey!" I lifted her legs and drilled her hard. Her moaning and groaning increased until it reached a crescendo, and she called out.

"Ahhhh! Ohhhhh! Damn! I'm coming, Dirk! Oh! Oh! Oh! Oh, I'm coming!" and then her body shuddered as she enjoyed the orgasm.

I wasn't quite there yet, and she recognized it at once. "Roll me over, Dirk! Do me from behind!" she gasped.

That was a great idea, so I pulled out. She deftly rolled over and got on all fours. I slid in behind her, and she guided my slimy cock home, with me pushing all the way in at once, to her gasp of pleasure. I held her by the waist and started a nice fast pumping, but I was tiring fast. I cranked up the energy for one last shot as she called out, "As hard as you want, Dirk!" I pounded away for a minute and then came all at once, shooting a load of cum deep within her. I stopped thrusting and stayed within her as she wiggled her ass back into me. I always liked that. That may have been worth an extra spurt. I was panting hard, and she called out for me to lie down, so I did.

I was on my back, breathing hard and sweating. She curled up against me and gently asked, "How are you doing, sweetie?"

I panted out, "You young women are going to kill me! But it's worth it."

"Ahem. That's a young woman, singular, shithead. But thanks for calling me young. You sure make me feel like a horny girl again."

"It's my pleasure. We'll have to do that again sometime."

She kissed me. "Anytime you want, amore mio."

"How about now?"

She laughed. "Yeah, right. How about when we get home?"

Last flight

In the morning, we went down for breakfast and found that Marco had set up a nice buffet for our crew in the party room. He grinned with pleasure as we exclaimed over the feast, fussing over us and ordering his staff about in staccato Italian if he thought we needed anything. Jim and our international relief pilot Duane joined us, and we had a nice long visit over coffee. Jess looked at her watch and declared that we needed to get ready, so we left the guys and some of the flight attendants who had wandered in.

Back in the room, Jess wanted to press my shirt and slacks, so I set up the ironing board for her while I watched the BBC news. When all was to her satisfaction, we got dressed, packed up, and looked at each other. I broke the silence. "Well, this is it." She nodded, and we checked our appearance in the mirror, and after Jess fussed over my tie, we left the suite and headed downstairs to meet the crew.

Strangely enough, the entire crew was present. I looked at my watch, we were 10 minutes early. I had never had the entire crew ready for the van early before. Amazing. The crew looked a little somber, so I decided to cheer them up, so I got their attention. "Thanks for a wonderful party and evening, everyone! Special thanks to Jess for setting it up. I'll find every one of you during the flight back to visit and say thanks in person. Now let's have a great flight back to Atlanta and have some fun!" They cheered up and were once again their noisy and chatty selves.

Everything was normal at the airport, and our plane had come in on time and was cleaned and fueled already. I looked over the flight plan with the other pilots, discussed the weather and fuel reserve, and then reached for my pen to sign the flight release and take command for the last time. I hesitated, and my hand shook as the pen hovered over my printed name on the paperwork. Jim was watching me. I looked up, and we locked eyes. He knew what was going through my head. He just smiled, and nodded his head, like Dirk, it's okay, man. Sign it. I signed the station copy and handed that to the agent, then handed our copies to Jim for entry into the flight management computer. The gate agent opened the door for us, and I headed down the jetbridge with my colleagues one last time.

The cabin crew was buzzing around doing their thing, and after I dropped my bags, I headed back to brief the crew. Jess looked at me and I nodded. She picked up the PA and announced, "Crew Briefing!" and all the flight attendants stopped what they were doing and came to the First Class section. With my briefing guide in my shaking hand, I calmly briefed the crew.

"All right, guys. We'll be ten and a half hours in the air today. The weather is great. We may get some turbulence around 20 degrees west or about four hours into the flight. Watch the seat belt sign, and if you think it's too rough, wedge your service carts in the aisle and jump into someone's lap. We'll use standard signals for evacuation or ditching. Any specials today, Jess?"

"We'll have five wheelchairs and about 10 lap babies. Nothing out of the ordinary."

"Thanks, Jess. As I said earlier, I'll be around to see every one of you during the flight. Thanks for being with me today. It means a lot to me." With that, I smiled and walked back to the flight deck.

Duane was getting his safety vest on to do the walk-around inspection. I stopped him. "I got it, Duane. Thanks." I wanted to walk around the plane for my last flight. He nodded in understanding. "Want me to check the flight plan entry?" I nodded and walked out the jetbridge door.

Outside, I slowly walked around the big Boeing, admiring her from every aspect. I checked all the required items, stuck my head in the engine inlets and exhaust that were still warm from the incoming flight, looked at the tires, brakes, and panels, and said hi to all the ground crew guys. I climbed the jetbridge stairs, worked the combination, and opened the door. Before stepping inside, I took one more look at the beautiful plane that had carried me faithfully across oceans and deserts. I shook my head and went in.

Passengers were already loading, and I heard the noisy chaos as everyone found their seats and stowed too much crap in the overhead bins. I passed Jess as she was talking to some first-class passengers, and we exchanged smiles. I got in my seat, adjusted the lumbar support and tilt, then reached for the pile of paperwork on the center console and got ready to fly.

High over the Atlantic about four hours later, we were near the area where turbulence was expected, so I turned the seat belt sign on. The Atlantic was its usual blue way down there, and I saw whitecaps indicating a strong wind at the surface. At least if we had to ditch it would be daylight. Jess came up with our dinner and handed trays to Jim and me. Duane was in the back on his FAA-mandated break. I looked at my tray and then at Jim's. "What the hell, Jess? One little piece of chicken and some veggies. Where's the dinner roll, potato, and my dessert?"

She was not sympathetic. "You ate too much last night, and the other flight attendants will probably feed you dessert when you are visiting."

"But, Jess ..."

"Tough shit, Caldwell. File a complaint with the company."

She left, and it was all Jim could do to keep from laughing out loud. I glared at him. "Give me half your roll."

He laughed. "No way! I'm not risking the wrath of Jess!"

An hour or so later, Duane came back up to relieve Jim. I would be taking the last break today. He climbed in, and Jim went to the back. Duane passed on, "Jess said for you to get out of your seat and stretch."

I looked at him malevolently. He held both hands up. "Hey, I'm just the messenger."

Sighing, I got up and stood behind my seat, and did some trunk twists and leg stretches. I was getting sore, it felt good to stand up.

Duane and I chatted, and he asked about some of the places I'd been and the experiences I had. He was a good cockpit buddy, with a good sense of humor, and more importantly, he knew when to shut up.

After a few hours, Jim came back up. I looked at him and said, "That was a short break."

"Yeah, I can't sleep during the day. I did some reading and was ready to come back up and look out the front."

I looked out at the seemingly endless ocean in front of us and nodded. "Nothing like it in the world."

Duane hopped out and hit the head while Jim got strapped in and I gave him the required changeover briefing. Duane was back, so I got out and watched while he got in and got squared away. I slapped each of them on the shoulder and said to let me know when we were coasting in. They gave a thumbs-up, and I went to the back.

Jess was in the first class galley doing something, with Nancy keeping her company while reading a magazine on the jump seat. I looked in the back, everyone was watching a movie, reading, or sleeping. We were between meal and beverage services, so I could make it to the back without a cart in the way. I stepped into the galley, and Jess looked at me with concern. "Hi! How's the back?"

"Pretty good. I got up and stretched as you ordered."

She smiled. "Nobody orders you around, Caldwell. I strongly suggest things."

I looked at Nancy for support. "See what kind of abuse I put up with?"

She held up her hands. "I'm not getting in the middle of anything with you two lovebirds."

Jess finished whatever she was doing. "Ready to go visiting?"

I nodded. She stopped me. "Will you take all those glasses off your neck? Sheesh." She reached up and fussed with my tie. "Okay."

We walked to the back, her leading the way. She still had a nice ass. We got to the back galley, and I always marveled at how much noisier it was back behind the wing with the engine exhaust noise. Several flight attendants were standing around the galley, and they all greeted me warmly. Darlene handed me a piece of pie. "I've been saving this for you. Want some coffee?"

I stood with them and nibbled on pie and sipped coffee, as we reminisced about old times.

Ann said, "Dirk, remember on 9/11 when you had everyone up to your room for a slumber party?"

I nodded. Jess perked up, that event had happened while we were split up and she hadn't heard about it. "What was that about?"

Chris chimed in. "We had been watching the news all day about the attack, and the video of the airliners crashing into the World Trade Center. They kept showing it over and over, and we were all bummed out. Dirk volunteered his room for everyone to come hang out and watch chick flicks and stay the night if we wanted. There must have been about six of us on his bed, all cuddled up and snuggly. Dirk was like a big brother, helping us out. I think I lay up against him most of the night with his arm around me. We ate snacks and drank wine, and he kept cracking us up with funny comments. It was a big help. I told my husband about it, and he was really appreciative that Dirk took care of us."

Ann said, "I think I was on his other side." She looked at Jess. "He's a really good snuggler."

Jess laughed and said that she knew that.

We got done visiting and I hugged everyone and told them I'd miss them. I got lots of kisses and we went to the business class galley. Roger was there, and several more flight attendants. He greeted me, "Hey Dirk. Want a hot fudge sundae? I saved one for you." I must have looked neglected. Jess gave me the look, but she did not say anything. "Thanks, Roger. Maybe I'll share it with Jess." She rolled her eyes.

He gave me a coffee as well, and we stood around visiting. Jess said, "I just heard a story about Dirk's slumber party on 9/11. Does anyone else have a good Dirk story?"

Evelyn spoke up. "I had a corner of the bed that night. Dirk really helped us out."

Jess looked at me with a funny smile. Then Roger spoke up.

"Dirk, remember that time we overnighted in Austin and we were all going to get a drink at the rooftop bar, then go to dinner?" I nodded, smiling. He turned to Jess. "We were in the lobby, heading up to the bar, and I invited the Captain to join us. He declined, then called Dirk off to the side to say something to him. They talked for a minute, and then the Captain got mad and stormed off. Dirk joined us and didn't say anything, and we all went to the bar. After a drink and us all chatting, one of the other guys asked Dirk why the Captain had stormed off in a huff. Dirk didn't want to tell us, but we made him. The Captain told Dirk he had better not hang out with three gay flight attendants, it would look bad. They had words, and then the Captain stormed off."

Jess looked at me. "What did you say to the Captain?"

I laughed. "I think I told him he was being a homophobic, bigoted asshole and a shitty human being. He wrote me up with the Chief Pilot office, saying I was insubordinate, and my morals were suspect."

We all laughed. Roger asked, "I never knew that. Did you get in trouble?"

"No. The Chief Pilot called me, I explained myself and they dropped it."

Roger looked at me. "Thanks for sticking up for us. I mean that."

"Anytime, Roger. We're all humans, everyone should be more tolerant and just be happy."

There were more stories and hugs, and then Jess and I went to the first-class galley. "No more dessert for you, Sarge. Damn! I'm hearing things about you I never heard before. Why don't I know these things?"

I shrugged. "I'm modest."

She got a good laugh out of that. Nancy came up from serving someone. "What's so funny?"

"Dirk said he was modest."

Nancy just looked at me and smiled. "A modest pilot. Now that's an oxymoron."

I tried to look offended. "I can feel the love here!"

Some passenger flagged Jess down, so she went to see what they needed, leaving Nancy and me alone in the galley. She said, "I told you 20 years ago to take good care of my flight attendant, Dirk."

"How'd I do?"

She smiled. "Jess is a bright, capable, talented, and now happy woman."

I nodded. "We've been through some rough times, but that's well in the past now."

"I know, Dirk. Jess and I have talked. I'm glad you two are happy together. You did take good care of my flight attendant. I'm grateful." She leaned over and kissed me on the cheek as Jess came back. She shook her head.

"Dirk's getting a lot of kisses today."

Nancy hugged me and smiled up at me. "And he deserves them, dear. Every flight attendant that asked to be on this trip has at least one very positive story about our Dirk, and how he has touched their lives in a good way."

I didn't know what to say.

Jess did. She scolded me, "You need to take a rest. I've got seat 1F for you, with 1E empty. Go sit down and try to get a nap."

I went and sat down and pulled up the screen showing the flight progress. We had about an hour before coasting in, I could watch a comedy show on the entertainment system until then.

After a while, I became aware that someone was leaning over me, and I felt a brush of lips on my forehead like someone kissed me. I opened my eyes and saw Jess's blue ones staring into mine as she smiled at me from a foot away. "Time to wake up, Dirk. Jim says we have 90 minutes to go."

I looked at the flight status display on the entertainment system. We were well on our way down the coast. "Damn it, I told them to get me up ..."

"Yes, my love. Jim called me about an hour ago and said we were at that point, and when I told him you were sleeping soundly, he said everything was fine and to wait another hour. You had a good nap, about two hours. You've got plenty of time to wake up before we descend."

I decided to be pleased. "Thanks, honey."

I stood up, stretched, and used the head before I went back up. Jess handed me my three sets of glasses to hang back around my neck. I put those on and said I was ready. Jess picked up the intercom, and said, "The Captain is ready to come up." They went through the security protocol and the flight deck door opened. I stepped up to the flight deck for the last time.

Landing and parking

I blinked in the bright afternoon sunlight and noticed that we were over the eastern seaboard. The pilots both turned around and smiled. I said, "Thanks for letting me get some extra sleep. Sorry to screw you guys out of your break." They both waved that off, and Duane asked if I was ready to get in my seat. I was.

I sat down, adjusted the seat, strapped in, looked at the flight plan, and got the briefing from Jim. I nodded, then said, "I have the airplane." I would be the sole manipulator of the controls from here to the gate. "Jim, I landed in Rome. How is your landing currency? Duane?" They both said they were current, and that I should take the landing. I nodded. "In that case, I'll take it." I was glad, but I've never been a stick hog. If they had needed it, I would have let them land.

We flew down the coast, bending in over North Carolina, and then air traffic control told us to begin our descent. I disconnected the autopilot and began to hand-fly the descent, feeling the airplane through my fingertips. I gave my welcome announcement over the PA and kept the descent steady, not wanting anyone in the back to feel any control inputs. Steadily descending for a west arrival, I kept the speed up and the rate of descent constant. As we passed 10,000 feet, I warned the flight attendants that we were about to land. Shortly after that, I heard the flight deck door open, and some conversation behind me. I looked over my shoulder, and Jess was there.

"Nancy is covering my position. We're legal." I looked over at Jim, who shrugged. I'm sure there was some rule about a flight attendant on the flight deck for landing, but it seemed nobody cared. Duane helped Jess get strapped into the jumpseat behind me. After a minute, she put her hand on my left shoulder. She whispered, "I've never seen you land!" I reached up and patted her hand, then went back to flying.

The west runways of Atlanta appeared about 15 miles ahead of us. I intercepted the glide slope and localizer path and called for the flaps and landing gear to be extended at the proper time. Soon the runway grew larger in my window. I could feel the airplane through the controls, she was talking to me, telling me where she wanted me to put the controls for the correct response. Then I heard the radio altimeter automatically counting down the last few feet of the descent. Don't screw this up now, Caldwell!

A mechanical voice started calling out the number of feet above the runway.

"50!"

"40!"

"30!" I pulled the thrust levers to idle.

"20!" After a heartbeat, I started to raise the nose a degree or so.

"10!" I looked down to the end of the runway to gauge the sink rate and added a hair of back pressure.

The main wheels touched down smoothly, then the auto-speed brakes deployed, but I still had to land the nose wheel. I made a micro release of the back pressure and raised the thrust reverser levers as the nose wheel settled to the ground without a jar. Both engines went into reverse thrust, and I started an easy push on the brakes. I could hear 200 passengers cheering loudly. That's unusual.

Jim called out, "80 knots!" and I pushed the reverse thrust levers to reverse idle.

He then called "60 knots!" so I stowed the reversers and reached for the nose wheel tiller.

The air traffic controller gave us taxi instructions to our ramp and then added, "Welcome home, Captain! Congrats on your retirement." I was surprised, did the whole world know?

I taxied the plane to the international terminal and was ready to pull into the gate when I saw a mob of people waiting at ground level. "What the hell?" Two fire trucks began spraying water high into the air as we passed, giving us the water cannon salute as we taxied under the arch of water. I looked over at Jim, who was grinning broadly, he had known about it. I lined up with the centerline stripe for gate F2 in the new international terminal, overshooting a little as I lined up the tail with the stripe. There were hundreds of people waving and yelling on the ramp, pilots, flight attendants, gate agents, mechanics, and ramp workers all greeting us. Some had signs, and there was a banner, "Congratulations Captain Dirk!" I was nearly overwhelmed with emotion. I waved back with my right hand, as my left was on the tiller. I called, "Everybody wave!" and they did. I quickly looked over my shoulder at Jess. Tears of joy were streaming down her cheeks while she was smiling and waving.

The ground handler gave me a slight correction, then slowly raised his wands together, then crossed them. I stopped the 767 without a jar, then set the parking brake. I looked to make sure the APU was running, turned off the seat belt sign, then moved the engine fuel control switches to cutoff. Jim extended his hand. "Another on-time arrival! Congratulations, Captain! Welcome home!"

We were home.

Don't miss out!

Visit the website below and you can sign up to receive emails whenever Dirk Caldwell publishes a new book. There's no charge and no obligation.

https://books2read.com/r/B-A-UHDZ-ECENC

BOOKS 2 READ

Connecting independent readers to independent writers.

Did you love *Flight Attendants want Love: Flying High with Jessica*?
Then you should read *Confessions of a Naughty Flight Attendant*[1] by
Jessica Jackson!

[2]

A hot story of a very naughty flight attendant. Flight attendant Jesssica
decides her life is too routine and conservative, so she decides to be
as naughty as she can. Join Jess as she explores sexual freedom and
gets increasingly more wild with her exploits and experimentation,
culminating in a sexy consensual bondage episode.

---

1. https://books2read.com/u/4jzdNk

2. https://books2read.com/u/4jzdNk

Also by Dirk Caldwell

Adventures of Stan
Stan does a Big Girl and gives her a Big Orgasm
Stan Does a Female Police Officer While On Duty
Stan Scores on a Booty Call with Barbara
Stan Takes Barb's Anal Cherry
Stan Teaches Oklahoma Karen About Sex in the City
Stan gets Kinky with Barb on Vacation
Barb Wants more Orgasms with Stan before She gets Engaged to
Another Man
Stan Does Barbara's Mom!

Dirk Caldwell Romantic Erotic Novels
A Visit to the Farm with Darla - a Sexy Short Story
A Layover in Omaha with Tina
A Night in Eufaula with Lynn
A Trip to the Lake with Kim
Older Women need Love, too! Erika visits Atlanta
Lessons in Love: Gabriella visits Indianapolis
Big Girls Need Love, too! Barbara from Kokomo
Flight Attendants want Love: Flying High with Jessica
Back to the Farm with Darla - A Sexy Sequel
Redheads need Love: Megan from New Orleans

A Big Girl finds Love: Joann from Shreveport
Lust from London: My Affair with a British Nymphomaniac
Paula's Sexy European Weekend
Mother and Daughter Threesome

Dirk Caldwell Sexy Short Stories
To All the Girls I've Loved Before: Sexy Short Stories Book 1
To All the Girls I've Loved Before: Sexy Short Stories Book 2
To All the Girls I've Loved Before: Sexy Short Stories Book 3

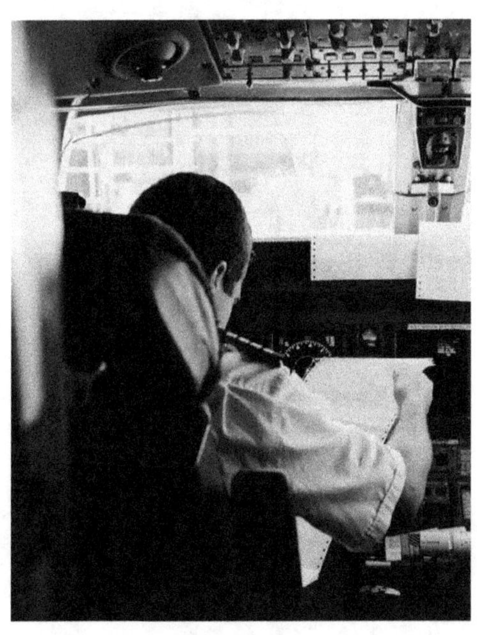

About the Author

Dirk Caldwell is the pen name of the author of an erotic book series. Dirk embodies the life experiences of the author as an Air Force veteran and commercial airline pilot. Most of the content is true and relates to the author's experiences. It's up to the reader to decide what is fiction and what is true life.